## "You need a bodyguard. If not for you, then for your son."

"I can protect him myself." God, she sounded foolish.

"Drive by here ———————— if I can spot anybo———————— as he walked her ———————— ind you, I promise.

She slanted a look at ———————— eal- ized just how hollow his promises sounded after what happened between them three years ago. Although he hadn't really made her any promises that night, had he? There hadn't been many words at all, just kisses and touches and a raging fire she'd thrown herself into without a second thought.

For him, it might have been nothing more than a few hours of shared grief and release.

But that night with Luke Cooper had changed her world.

# PAULA GRAVES

# ONE TOUGH MARINE

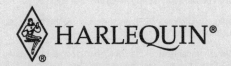

HARLEQUIN®

TORONTO • NEW YORK • LONDON
AMSTERDAM • PARIS • SYDNEY • HAMBURG
STOCKHOLM • ATHENS • TOKYO • MILAN • MADRID
PRAGUE • WARSAW • BUDAPEST • AUCKLAND

If you purchased this book without a cover you should be aware
that this book is stolen property. It was reported as "unsold and
destroyed" to the publisher, and neither the author nor the
publisher has received any payment for this "stripped book."

For Ashlee, my *Psych* viewing buddy.
Bum-bum-bum...muffins!

Recycling programs
for this product may
not exist in your area.

ISBN-13: 978-0-373-69491-4

ONE TOUGH MARINE

Copyright © 2010 by Paula Graves

All rights reserved. Except for use in any review, the reproduction or
utilization of this work in whole or in part in any form by any electronic,
mechanical or other means, now known or hereafter invented, including
xerography, photocopying and recording, or in any information storage
or retrieval system, is forbidden without the written permission of the
publisher, Harlequin Enterprises Limited, 225 Duncan Mill Road,
Don Mills, Ontario, Canada M3B 3K9.

This is a work of fiction. Names, characters, places and incidents are
either the product of the author's imagination or are used fictitiously,
and any resemblance to actual persons, living or dead, business
establishments, events or locales is entirely coincidental.

This edition published by arrangement with Harlequin Books S.A.

For questions and comments about the quality of this book please contact
us at Customer_eCare@Harlequin.ca.

® and TM are trademarks of the publisher. Trademarks indicated with
® are registered in the United States Patent and Trademark Office, the
Canadian Trade Marks Office and in other countries.

www.eHarlequin.com

**Printed in U.S.A.**

## ABOUT THE AUTHOR

Alabama native Paula Graves wrote her first book, a mystery starring herself and her neighborhood friends, at the age of six. A voracious reader, Paula loves books that pair tantalizing mystery with compelling romance. When she's not reading or writing, she works as a creative director for a Birmingham advertising agency and spends time with her family and friends. She is a member of Southern Magic Romance Writers, Heart of Dixie Romance Writers and Romance Writers of America.

Paula invites readers to visit her Web site, www.paulagraves.com.

### Books by Paula Graves

Don't miss any of our special offers. Write to us at the following address for information on our newest releases.

Harlequin Reader Service
U.S.: 3010 Walden Ave., P.O. Box 1325, Buffalo, NY 14269
Canadian: P.O. Box 609, Fort Erie, Ont. L2A 5X3

# CAST OF CHARACTERS

*Abby Chandler*—When masked men threaten to hurt her son if the marine widow can't give them what they want, Abby turns to Luke Cooper, her late husband's best friend—and the unwitting father of her son.

*Luke Cooper*—Retired from the Marine Corps, Luke lives in self-exile to protect the ones he loves from a ruthless drug lord's vow of vengeance.

*Stevie Chandler*—The two-year-old has become a pawn in a deadly game of extortion.

*Eladio Cordero*—When Luke killed the South American drug kingpin's only son, Cordero vowed to make him pay by going after the people who mean the most to Luke.

*Los Tiburones*—Cordero's hired enforcers have caught Luke's scent, dogging his trail, leaving death and destruction in their wake.

*Barton Reid*—His job high in the U.S. State Department has given him access to a great deal of power and volatile information. He'll go to any lengths to protect his secrets.

*Demetrius "Damon" Miles*—An operative in Barton Reid's private army, Damon has his own hidden agenda.

*Sam Cooper*—Luke's older brother is the only Cooper who knows the truth about Luke's self-imposed exile. Can Sam help Luke and Abby reach safety before the bad guys catch up?

# Chapter One

Abby Chandler shifted the grocery bag to her left arm and fumbled in her pocket for her keys. Arriving home later than she'd planned, thanks to a pileup on I-5, she had to hurry and put away the groceries so she could pick up Stevie by six. After six Mrs. Tamburello charged time and a half, and the budget this month couldn't take the strain.

She unlocked her apartment and pushed the door open with her foot, stumbling as her toe caught on the rubber welcome mat inside. Muttering a curse, she kicked the door shut behind her and took a half step forward before she realized what she was seeing in the dim afternoon light filtering into her apartment.

Sofa cushions, ripped apart and tossed on the floor. Paintings torn from the wall and dismantled. Her coffee table upended in the middle of the room.

Her heartbeat barely had time to notch upward when a voice, inches from her ear, sent it hurtling into hyperdrive.

"You're late, Mrs. Chandler."

At the sound of the deep male voice, her body jerked into one jangling nerve. Her keys dropped with a clatter from her numb fingers while her mind flew haphazardly through her options. Run? No, the man with the deep voice stood between her and the door. Try to outrace him to the kitchen for the knife block by the refrigerator? Not a chance.

"Sorry for the mess. We became bored waiting for you." A second voice, not quite as deep as the first, spoke to her right. She heard more than a hint of Boston Brahmin in that accent.

"What do you want?" She felt her grip on the grocery bag slipping and tucked it to her side to keep from dropping it.

"Please don't move, Mrs. Chandler," the man behind her said. "We don't want things here to escalate."

*Escalate to what—unadulterated terror? Too late, buster.*

The second man moved into her field of vision—tall, well built, dressed in black from his soft-soled shoes to his knit ski mask. Clear blue eyes, direct and confident, gazed out from the eyeholes. He was light-skinned, with a hint of freckles, she noted for future reference.

Assuming there'd be a future in which to reference.

"Are you going to tell me what you want?" She tried not to give in to the panic buzzing like wasps in her brain. Her muscles were already beginning to ache from tension. If someone didn't start talking, she might just snap in half.

The freckled man took the grocery bag from her trembling arms and set it on the floor. "Your husband took something that didn't belong to him. We're here to retrieve it."

The man behind her pushed something cold and hard against the back of her neck. It took no imagination to guess it was the barrel of a pistol.

"My husband's been dead for three years. Most of his stuff has been sold or given away." Her answer had the benefit of being the truth. Matt hadn't collected much in the way of personal belongings during his foreshortened life. Most of what he possessed had been government issue, from uniforms to gear to weapons. "If you've been through the trunk at the foot of my bed, you've seen all I have left of him."

The Brahmin, as she thought of him, made a low *tsk-tsk*

sound. "Perhaps you are mistaken. Did your husband have a safe-deposit box? A storage unit located elsewhere?"

"I don't know," she answered, and again it was the truth. "He was a soldier. There was a lot about his life I don't know. Can you at least tell me what this is about? Maybe I could help you find what you're looking for if you told me what it was."

The Brahmin hesitated a moment. She caught a slight flicker in his eyes and realized he wasn't sure how to answer.

*Oh, God, they don't even know what they're looking for.*

"We're not at liberty to reveal that to you if you don't already know what we're talking about," the man behind her said, and she almost laughed at the absurdity. They'd broken in and trashed her apartment on a hunch that maybe, possibly, her husband had hidden—what? A million dollars? A stash of gold?

"We're looking for files." The Brahmin's accent slipped, she noticed. He might be playing the role of the upper-crust Bostonian, but for just a moment he sounded more like a South Boston street punk. His Brahmin accent clicked back into place almost immediately. "Of a sensitive nature. Your husband took them from an associate of ours who wants them back immediately."

"Paper files? Digital?" The growing discomfort of her captors had begun to ease her own sense of terror. If they didn't know what, precisely, they were looking for, maybe she could buy time to get herself out of this mess. "My husband's personal notebook computer is in the closet. It stopped booting up a year ago, but maybe you could get something off of it."

"We have it. We'll certainly examine it," the Brahmin said. "But what we're looking for won't be on a computer. Your husband was too smart to keep it in such an obvious place."

He was right, of course. Matt had been the king of secret-keepers. It had come with his career in Marine Corps

Intelligence. God knew, she'd had to get used to being out of the loop when it came to the biggest part of his life.

"If you knew my husband at all, you'd know he didn't share his work with me." By the end, there'd been little they'd shared besides a house and a few good memories.

"That's unfortunate," the Brahmin said. Behind her, the man with the gun pushed the barrel more firmly against her neck.

The unnatural calm that had briefly settled over her shattered. When she spoke again, her voice shook. "I don't know what you want from me."

"I suggest you find out," the Brahmin said. "Assuming you enjoy your life with your adorable little boy."

The mention of Stevie made her heart skip. "What do you mean by that?"

"Mrs. Tamburello is getting along in years, wouldn't you say? Accidents can happen so easily."

"Where's Stevie?" Ignoring the man with the gun behind her, she rushed forward and grabbed the Brahmin's arm. "If you've done anything to him, I'll—"

"Rage impotently?" the Brahmin said dismissively.

"You son of a bitch!"

"Your son is well. Mrs. Tamburello is well." The Brahmin motioned with his head, and the man behind her grabbed her arm.

She wheeled around to face him and found another masked man, slightly shorter than the Brahmin. African-American, judging by the café au lait skin visible through the eyeholes, along with intelligent brown eyes that met hers with surprising gentleness. Nevertheless, he held her gaze unflinchingly, slowly lifting the pistol he held in his right hand as if to remind her who was in charge. A Colt M1991, stainless with a black grip, .45 caliber. Nasty piece of work.

She ought to be panicking instead of noticing the details

of a pistol, but the fact that she was still alive after this much time alone with two masked men suggested she might not be dying today. It was in her best interest to remember as much about these two men as she could.

The Brahmin tapped her shoulder, making her jump. She whipped around to face him. "Here is what we're going to do, Mrs. Chandler. You are going to go into your bedroom and close the door behind you. My associate and I will take the items we've collected and leave. When you hear the door close behind us, you may come out of the room."

"Then what?" she asked, knowing it couldn't be that simple.

"Then you will collect your thoughts and memories until you come up with an answer to a very important question. Where would your husband hide sensitive material to keep it out of the hands of his employers as well as any other interested parties?"

Her heart dropped. "And if I come up empty-handed?"

"You will lose your son in a dreadful accident."

She clenched her fists so hard her fingernails bit into her palms. "If you think I'm going to let anyone hurt my son—"

The Brahmin took a leisurely step toward her. "Do you not understand you really have no choices here? A call to the police, an attempt to leave San Diego—any of those things will be met with punishment. You have one simple task. Find what your husband hid. Deliver it to us by the end of the week and we will leave you and your son alone."

"Liar."

"On the contrary. I've spoken only the truth today." The Brahmin reached out and touched a strand of hair that had slipped from her ponytail. "If you trust nothing else, trust that. I will do what I promised, either way. The outcome is entirely up to you."

Behind her, the man with the Colt nudged her neck with the barrel. "Get into the bedroom."

Swallowing the anger rising in her throat, she walked slowly through the upended living room and entered her tiny bedroom, dismay settling over her like a cloud as she took in the shredded mattress and ransacked drawers. Behind her, the door closed, shutting her in.

She leaned against the bedroom door, tears leaking from her eyes as she waited for the sound of the front door closing. A few seconds later, she heard the door click shut.

But she didn't move right away. Her shaking knees wouldn't hold her weight.

*Damn you, Matt. Damn your secrets and lies.*

After a couple of seconds, the need to see her son overcame her shattered nerves. She left the bedroom and located her keys on the floor near the front door, where she'd dropped them. To her surprise, the men had set her bag of groceries on the dining-nook table before they left. Polite bastards.

As she raced up the steps to the second floor, where Mrs. Tamburello lived, she tried to make sense of what had just happened. Who were those men? From the look and sound of them, she'd say ex-military. The posture was always a give-away. The Colt M1991 was also a military style of pistol. They'd taken her under control with ease, also suggesting armed-forces training.

So—mercenaries? Private security operatives? If they were working in an official capacity, they wouldn't have had to sneak around. They'd have simply taken her into custody.

Abby paused at Mrs. Tamburello's door, taking a moment to slow her rapid breathing. She didn't want to scare Stevie. It was going to be bad enough taking him back to their trashed apartment. She knocked on the door and stepped back, smoothing her hair and praying she looked calmer than she felt.

Mrs. Tamburello opened the door with a harried smile. "I

was about to call you to see where you'd gotten to," she said, waving Abby inside the warm apartment.

"Mama!" Stevie met her before she'd made it two feet inside, wrapping his little arms around her knees. She swung him up into her arms, squeezing him tightly, her pulse pounding in her head. He smelled like peanut butter and chocolate milk. She fought the urge to cry again.

"Traffic was crazy," she murmured against his silky hair, smiling apologetically at Mrs. Tamburello. "Was he a handful?"

"Not at all." Mrs. Tamburello flashed Stevie an affectionate smile. "You're a good boy, aren't you, Stephen?"

Stevie nodded, his gray eyes solemn. "I maded kitty."

Mrs. Tamburello chuckled and retrieved a piece of paper from the coffee table. It was a scribble of bright colors, vaguely in the shape of…something. The oranges and yellows suggested her two-year-old son had tried his hand at capturing Mrs. Tamburello's scruffy yellow tabby in crayon.

Abby took the drawing from Mrs. Tamburello and shifted Stevie to her left hip. "Thank you, Mrs. Tamburello. I'm taking the next couple of days off, so you'll have an extra-long weekend." Remembering the words of her captors, she added, "Maybe you should drive up to see your sister in Temecula."

Mrs. Tamburello smiled, obviously pleased that Abby had remembered that detail about her family. "Perhaps I will. She has a brand-new grandbaby, you know."

"Yes, I know," Abby said, hoping she'd take the suggestion. The two men in her apartment meant business. Abby didn't doubt they'd hurt Mrs. Tamburello to make their point.

She dug in her pocket for Mrs. Tamburello's salary for the week, adding an extra ten. *Guilt money for putting the woman in danger,* she supposed grimly as she made her way back down the stairs with Stevie clinging to her back like a little monkey.

He eyed the mess in the living room for half a second before tugging at her hair from behind. "I hungwy."

She swung him over her shoulders into her arms, looking into his big gray eyes. The quizzical look on his sweet face brought back a rush of poignant memories.

*Large, gentle hands, cradling her face. A deep, warm voice, still lightly graced with the liquid drawl of his native South, whispering words of comfort and passion.*

Realization washed over her, producing relief and dread in equal parts. Luke. Of course. If anyone had known Matt Chandler's secrets, it had been his best friend, Luke Cooper. But was Luke even in San Diego anymore? The last she'd heard, almost a year ago, he'd resigned his commission from the Marine Corps shortly after he returned from overseas. Maybe one of her old friends from her Marine wife days would know where to find him.

"Tell you what, scooter," she said to Stevie, her voice settling into the familiar Texas twang of her youth, "how about we go to McDonald's for dinner?" *While Mama makes an important phone call,* she added silently.

Stevie patted her face with delight. "McDonald's! McDonald's!"

Promising herself to buy him yogurt instead of fries, she lowered him to the floor and led him outside to her car.

MALKIN SECURITY International was one of San Diego's most prestigious security firms, with a reputation for complete discretion and a track record of successful security operations in over fifty global hot spots. Their proximity to four Southern California military bases was no coincidence; they recruited heavily from the Marine and Naval bases and air stations in the area when they were looking for new employees.

Luke Cooper had worked at MSI for almost a year now, ever since he hung up his combat boots for life as a civilian. It wasn't nearly as exciting as the recruiting brochure had made it out to be, but if he'd wanted a nonstop adrenaline rush, he'd have stuck with the Marine Corps.

And working at Malkin also afforded him a certain level of personal security he couldn't afford to do without these days.

His current assignment had come to an end late that afternoon, when he had turned over all of his investigative materials to the police department in Rancho Santa Fe. They'd taken into custody a relentless stalker who'd been terrorizing a banker's nineteen-year-old daughter, and Luke had earned MSI—and himself—a hefty bonus for providing actionable evidence for the legal proceedings.

The girl had been nice enough, if pampered within an inch of her life, and the stalker had been escalating well past annoying into dangerous territory. Plus, Luke had been able to spend a lot of time at the banker's ranch, escorting the daughter on rambling horseback rides. As far as security jobs went, he'd seen worse.

At least nobody was shooting at him this time.

He filed the last of his paperwork around 7:00 p.m. and took a moment to scan the newspaper he'd bought that afternoon on the way into the office. For the past week and a half, there'd been rumblings that federal investigators were close to an indictment against a U.S.-based nongovernmental organization for illegal arms trading.

The articles had yet to identify the NGO by name, but Luke had a pretty good idea. The investigation of Voices for Villages had been the last thing he'd been working on before his retirement from the Marine Corps.

Still nothing official, he noted, folding the paper and tossing it in the trash. As he took the employee exit stairs down to the parking deck, he wondered what the snag was in making the case against Voices for Villages. People had died getting the evidence that implicated the NGO in a deadly drugs-for-arms racket.

He reached his car, a gunmetal-gray Ford Mustang, unlocked it and slid behind the wheel. It ran like a dream and turned more than a few female—and male—heads when he drove down the streets of San Diego, but recently he'd been thinking about buying a truck. Most of his brothers drove trucks back home in Chickasaw County, Alabama, he remembered, smiling. He guessed his kid sister, Hannah, did, too, now that she'd married a cowboy.

Guilt tugged at him, erasing his smile. He'd missed Hannah's wedding last year, although his mother had made sure to send him a couple of flash drives full of pictures from the event. He'd told his sister he was too involved in a case to leave San Diego even for a few days, but it had been a lie. There wasn't a case in the world that could've kept him from watching his baby sister get married.

Only Eladio Cordero could do that.

He shoved away the thought of Cordero with brutal determination. There wasn't anything he could do about Cordero's threat until the South American drug lord finally decided to make his move. If U.S. law enforcement or the Sanselmo authorities could have located the elusive thug, he'd be dead already. Worrying about it only kept him from focusing on the things he had to deal with day to day.

Like finding a better way to fill his long, lonely hours away from the job. Because it wasn't Eladio Cordero who haunted him in the still of the night, when sleep wouldn't come fast enough.

That honor belonged to Abby.

She would visit him tonight. She always did. He'd never been able to get drunk enough to escape her, and she always followed him into his dreams. Lately, he'd given up trying not to think about her and started looking forward to the nights he spent wrapped up in his memories of her. It was as close as he could ever let himself get, these days.

But it hadn't always been that way.

He exited the interstate on Genesee Avenue, heading south into University City, where he rented a one-story stucco with a two-car garage that was almost as large as the house itself. It wasn't much of a home, but the rent was reasonable, the neighbors quiet and the commute to work manageable.

These days, if he could live life with a minimum of fuss, he counted it as a win.

A beeping noise broke the silence inside the Mustang. Luke's breath hitched as he pulled his cell phone from his pocket. Red letters flashed on the black display.

*INTRUDER.*

In the span of a heartbeat, Luke's body went on high alert. He pulled the Glock from his hip holster and checked the clip. He was only a couple of minutes from home—should he call in backup? He wasn't sure he could trust anyone anymore. Not here in San Diego, anyway.

He was better off on his own.

Daylight lingered outside as he reached his house and parked by the curb in front. Scanning the street, he noticed a strange car parked a few houses away. Possibly a friend of the teenagers who lived down the street. But maybe not.

His garage provided cover from the street to the house. He stayed close to the building, moving as quietly as possible across the rocky ground to the side entrance of the house. The curtains in the kitchen window were closed, he noted. He always left them open.

Someone was definitely in the house.

He hunkered down at the side door and examined the lock. No sign of any tool marks on the dead bolt, but he knew there were other ways in. He hadn't tried to turn his house into a fortress once he became aware of Eladio Cordero's threats. He didn't want to live his life in a prison of his own making, for one thing. Hell, he was at a point now where he welcomed an attempt on his life, just to get it over with. He couldn't even risk a quick trip home to his family, thanks to the danger.

Cordero's vow of vengeance had been hanging over him long enough. He'd had all he could stand.

Quietly, he let himself inside the kitchen and stood still a moment, listening. He saw nothing out of place in the kitchen, nor did he hear anything beyond the normal hum of electrical appliances inside and faint traffic noise outside. But he caught a whiff of a strange scent—sweet, a little powdery. There was also a heaviness in the air, as if whoever lurked inside the dark recesses of the tiny bungalow was waiting just as he was, still and breathless, for another sound.

He tightened his grip on the Glock, slid off his shoes as quietly as possible and padded in sock-clad silence into the hallway, where he paused to listen.

To his left, where an open doorway led into the living room, he heard a faint snuffling sound. But before he could turn to enter, a ball of pure energy slammed into him from the bedroom, knocking him into the wall.

He caught a glimpse of wavy brown hair disappearing around the corner into the living room. Scrambling up, he took chase, catching up halfway to the narrow sofa against the wall. He took in a slim waist and nicely rounded backside before he whirled the intruder around to face him.

Cornflower-blue eyes met his, wide and scared. A smattering of coppery freckles dotted her peaches-and-cream complexion. Soft coral lips, as tempting as they'd ever been, parted to release a soft, shaky breath.

"Abby?" he breathed, his whole body tingling with surprise

and a darker, richer sensation he'd thought he'd buried three years ago, never to be exhumed.

Had he lost his mind? Had he conjured her up from the fabric of his memories and his longing?

Her gaze softened at the sound of his voice. A hint of guilt flashed in her eyes, then disappeared as desperation took hold of her expression, even as she plastered on a bright, brittle smile.

"Hi, Luke," she said. "Long time, no see."

## Chapter Two

Abby gazed into Luke Cooper's familiar face, fighting tears. Despite the disastrous end to their once-close relationship, Luke Cooper had been her best friend once.

And on one bleak, emotional night, he'd become her lover.

She tamped down her sentimental thoughts with ruthless efficiency. Her world had changed since they'd last spoken. And Luke had been nowhere around when she'd needed him the most.

She'd be a fool to forget that fact.

"What the hell are you doing here?" Luke lowered the Glock he'd pulled and slipped it into the holster at his hip. "How did you get in?"

"I knocked," she said in a feeble attempt at a joke. "I might have broken your bathroom window, too."

A snuffling sound behind her drew Luke's gaze to the sofa, where she'd left Stevie napping while she searched Luke's house.

Luke's gaze darted back to meet hers. "Yours?"

She nodded, holding her breath. Would he figure it out?

And did she want him to?

"What's his name?"

"Stephen. I call him Stevie." It had been Matt's father's name. After she'd discovered she was pregnant so soon after

Matt's funeral, everyone assumed he was the father. She'd let everyone believe the assumption; it was easier than the truth.

But Luke knew there was another possibility, didn't he?

Luke frowned. "You brought your kid on a B and E?"

"Thought I might need backup." She kept her voice light to hide the fact that she was feeling a little bit crazy and a whole lot desperate at the moment.

"What were you looking for?" he asked.

"I'm not sure." It was stupid to flail around blindly while the clock was ticking on her son's life. She should have contacted him directly as soon as an old Marine wife friend told her Luke was still living in San Diego, fifteen minutes away. This cloak-and-dagger rot was for the birds.

She just hadn't been ready to see him again. And judging by the tremors rocking through her at the moment, she still wasn't ready.

"Abs, what's wrong? You're shaking like a drunk in rehab."

"Matt took something from somebody," she blurted. "Somebody pretty damned big and powerful."

Luke's eyes narrowed. "Took what?"

"I don't know!" She pressed her hands to her throbbing temples. "I don't think they know, either. It's like they're on some fishing expedition and I'm the bait."

"You have no idea who they are?"

Behind her, their raised voices had awakened Stevie. He whimpered, unsettled by the unfamiliar setting and the strange man growling at his mother. Abby ignored Luke's question and hurried to her son. Stevie clung tightly to her, his yogurt-sticky fingers tangling in her hair. "Shh, baby, Mama's okay."

"Beautiful kid," Luke murmured. "Looks like you."

The tears she'd been fighting spilled down her cheeks.

"They threatened him, Luke. If I don't find whatever it was Matt hid, they'll kill Stevie."

Luke's eyes widened with alarm. "They threatened him?"

"They were waiting for me in my apartment when I got home from work. Two men." She sat down, no longer trusting her trembling legs to keep her upright. Luke shoved a couple of magazines aside and sat on the heavy wood coffee table in front of her. "They said Matt had stolen something important and they wanted it back. By the end of this week."

Luke's expression darkened.

She continued. "One spoke with a Boston Brahmin accent—but it slipped once, so I think he assumed the accent. The other guy came across as educated. A hint of a southern urban accent—probably born in a southern city but lost the accent."

Luke's lips curved, and she realized she was rattling on about linguistic cues in the middle of the biggest crisis of her life. "Some things never change," he murmured.

"Everything changes," she replied darkly. "I'm pretty sure these guys are ex-military, officer rank. SEALs or Rangers, maybe Special Forces—guys who came from tough neighborhoods but took advantage of the training and education. These aren't goons. Whatever I'm up against, it's big."

Luke muttered a profanity, then shot an apologetic look at Stevie. "How does Matt figure in?" he asked, though he didn't sound that surprised by what she was saying.

"I was hoping you'd know," she said. "You know he didn't tell me anything about his work."

"This wasn't work," Luke said quietly.

Her heart sank. She pressed her face against Stevie's soft cheek. "Then what?"

"The timing is interesting," Luke added thoughtfully.

Did Luke know what Matt had hidden or where to find it? "You know something."

"I don't *know* anything."

"But you have suspicions?"

Luke didn't meet her eyes when he answered. "He was spending time with people I didn't trust. People we came in contact with in the field."

Abby realized what he meant. "A woman."

Luke looked up sharply.

She smiled without humor. "I know he cheated on me. If that's what you're trying to hide—"

"Her name is Janis Meeks. Ran field ops for an organization called Voices for Villages."

"They fund and supply infrastructure construction in Sanselmo's poverty-stricken areas, right?"

"She and Matt—" Luke rubbed the back of his neck. "We suspected she was involved in something very bad, so I asked Matt to stay away from her. I guess he didn't."

By now, Abby realized, she shouldn't be surprised at discovering another one of her late-husband's infidelities. Matt had spent a year in the South American country, his intel unit attached to a peacekeeping unit assigned to the struggling democracy after a coup attempt. Matt hadn't been the type of man to go a year without sex. In fact, danger would have been an aphrodisiac.

After Sanselmo, he'd begun keeping secrets at every level of their relationship. The beginning of the end.

"Sanselmo was hell," Luke said bluntly. "Lots of bad things went down after the attempted coup. Marines died."

"I know," Abby murmured, distracted by Stevie wriggling in her grasp. She turned him in her lap to face Luke.

Luke smiled at Stevie. "Hi, big guy. My name is Luke. I knew your daddy."

Abby tried not to flinch. "I haven't told him much about Matt. He's not old enough to realize something's missing."

Stevie touched a small gold pendant in the shape of a hawk that hung from Luke's neck. "Bird."

Luke looked down at the sticky fingers tugging his necklace. "That's right, it's a big bird."

Abby smiled. She'd given the pendant to Luke for his birthday almost six years ago. Hawk was Luke's unit nickname. It had fit—strong, smart and always watching out for the people he cared for.

"I have to have some clue what he was into, Luke." She stroked Stevie's hair, shuddering at the memory of the masked man's threat. "They told me if I go to the cops, Stevie will suffer. I can't risk it."

"Sons of bitches." Luke's lips thinned to an angry line. "I think I know who they are, Abs—who they work for. But I swear, I don't know what they want you to find. If I knew, I'd give it to you."

"Tell me what you do know, then." She laid her hand on his arm. "This is what you'd call a need-to-know situation."

He sighed. "In Sanselmo, we were looking into American involvement in a drugs-for-arms black market. Some Sanselmano national guardsmen were trading government-issue arms and ordnance to *El Cambio* rebels in exchange for cocaine."

"Is that how they got so close to pulling off the coup?"

Luke nodded. "*El Cambio* has controlled the coca production in Sanselmo for decades—only game in town. A lot of money up for grabs. Worse, there were American arms found during raids."

"No way Matt was involved with trading arms for drugs," Abby said bluntly.

"Maybe not. But his connection to Janis Meeks—"

Abby winced at the mention of the woman's name. She'd

taken a few body blows over the months after Matt's death, as one story after another came to light.

Other Marine wives had warned her infidelity was common—part of the fog of war—and assured her that what happened overseas during a long tour of duty didn't have anything to do with Abby or with Matt's love for her. But she knew better.

Besides, since Sanselmo, she was pretty sure Matt had been cheating on her stateside, too.

"Matt might not have realized what he was facilitating," Luke continued. "The timing is interesting because the Feds are on the verge of indictments against Voices for Villages. Maybe Matt had something incriminating on Meeks or her organization that's coming to light now because of the impending charges."

"Like what?"

"That's the question." His gaze on Stevie's fingers fumbling with his pendant, Luke changed topics. "Why didn't you tell me you were pregnant that night after the funeral?"

"Would it have made a difference?"

His expression reflected guilt and regret. "I guess not."

She looked away, the memory of that night as vivid in her mind now as it had been the very next morning, when she'd awakened to find Luke had gone, leaving her with nothing but a note on the pillow and a little life growing inside her.

What if she'd put a call in to his unit overseas when she'd gotten the results of the pregnancy test? He couldn't have left Kaziristan to race to her side and play daddy to a baby he never intended to make. And she'd have never wanted him to feel obligated to be with her just because they made a baby together.

But what about now? Didn't Luke deserve to know that the little boy she was trying so desperately to protect from her husband's past was his own flesh and blood?

"I don't know what to do," she said aloud.

"Where is your car parked?" Luke asked, the question catching her off balance.

"About a block down the street. We walked from there."

He frowned. "You don't drive a dark blue Pontiac G-3?"

She shook her head. "Silver Honda Prelude."

Luke crossed to the front window. Parting the curtains about an inch, he peered outside, where the sun was making a last dying stand against twilight.

"Is someone out there?" Abby asked.

"Not anymore," he answered tersely. "But we have to assume they're around here somewhere, just to be safe."

The urge to cry returned, but she fended it off. She didn't have time for tears. "What should I do, Luke?"

"Right now, we don't have a clue what Matt might have taken, or where he'd have hidden it. If he took anything at all." He let the curtain drop and turned to her. "Right?"

She nodded. "I'm sure he had a dozen places he could stash something he wanted to hide, but he never shared that kind of information with me."

He came to stand in front of her, capturing her chin with his fingers and giving a little tug to make her look up at him. "I have some thoughts on that, but right now, let's get you and Little Bit home safely. You two can get a good night's sleep while I look into some hiding places Matt might have used."

The thought of returning to her mess of an apartment was almost more than she could bear, but she hid her despair from Luke. She wasn't about to start leaning on anyone again, no matter how broad and tempting the shoulders.

"I need your address. You're not staying at your apartment alone tonight," Luke said.

"Wait—" Panic rose in her gut in greasy waves. No way

was she sharing her tiny apartment with Luke Cooper while he played knight in shining armor. "I don't need a babysitter."

"You need a bodyguard." His tone was so reasonable she wanted to punch him. "If not for you, then for Stevie."

"I can protect him myself." God, she sounded foolish. Sure, she knew how to use a gun, but she didn't have one in the house because of Stevie. And while she was physically fit and knew a few self-defense moves that might get her out of trouble if some jerk tried to mug her on the street, she couldn't outfight two military-trained enforcers armed with Colt .45s.

"It won't hurt to have backup, right?" Luke crossed to a desk near the entryway and pulled a pen and notepad from one of the drawers. He wrote something, tore out the page and handed it to her. "My cell-phone number. I'll be a couple of minutes behind you, but call if you need anything."

"I will." She gave him her address as she rose, shifting Stevie to her hip. Luke jotted it down on another piece of paper.

"Drive by here on your way out and I'll see if I can spot anybody tailing you," Luke suggested as he walked her to the door. "I'll be right behind you, I promise."

She slanted a look at him, wondering if he realized just how hollow his promises sounded after what happened between them three years ago. Although he hadn't really made her any promises that night, had he? There hadn't been many words at all, just kisses and touches and a raging fire she'd thrown herself into without a second thought.

For him, it might have been nothing more than a few hours of shared grief and release.

But that night with Luke Cooper had changed her world.

"NOTHING UNDER THE NAME Matt Randall, either?" Luke asked the bus-station attendant on the phone, using one of the aliases Matt had used undercover with Marine Corps Intelligence.

"No, sir."

"Thanks anyway." Luke rang off and scanned the traffic around him, looking for any sign of a tail. He'd seen no one tailing Abby, but that didn't mean someone wasn't watching.

He spotted Abby's silver Honda a few car lengths ahead and his stomach turned a flip. Even tired, scared and frustrated, Abby Chandler was as beautiful as he'd remembered.

And even more off-limits now than when he first realized he was in love with Matt Chandler's wife.

Evening traffic was busy. Though he'd called San Diego home for the past seven years, he'd spent much of that time overseas and on assignments out of town. Only life as a civilian had allowed him to really get to know the place. It wasn't a bad place to live. The zoo was world-famous, Sea World a fun way to spend a lazy Saturday and the place was crawling with military personnel. But now that he was out of the Corps, he found himself thinking of his real home more and more.

He missed the green mountains of Chickasaw County, Alabama, the sparkling waters of Gossamer Lake and his mother's cooking. Now that his brother Sam was back in Alabama after years away, Luke was the last Cooper in exile.

Even with Eladio Cordero's threats hanging over him, the call of home was strong these days.

He wondered what Abby would think of Gossamer Ridge, Alabama, with its ten stoplights and one decent grocery store. He squelched that thought ruthlessly, aware how dangerous it was to think of Abby as anything but his old friend's widow.

He'd made a mistake three years ago, taking advantage of her grief and vulnerability to assuage his own. It didn't matter that he loved her; Abby had been Matt's wife. And now, the mother of the only child Matt Chandler would ever have.

And it just might be Luke's fault that Matt wasn't there to see his son grow up.

Stevie looked like Abby, from his freckles to his wide, expressive mouth. Not a hint of Matt's laughing brown eyes or olive complexion. Was it easier for Abby that way, not to have to see Matt in Stevie's eyes every time she looked at him?

How old was the kid now—two? Two and a half? No more than that; if Abby had been more than three or four months pregnant the night they spent together, he'd have noticed.

His smile faded suddenly.

What if she *hadn't* been pregnant that night? He tried to remember how she'd answered his questions about Stevie. Had she ever said, outright, that Matt was Stevie's father?

A chill washed over him. They hadn't used protection that night; they were too far gone to think about stopping for something like that. Neither of them had been thinking about pregnancy.

But she'd have told him. Abby wasn't a secret-keeper like he and Matt had been. She'd been open, sharing her thoughts and feelings with abandon. It had been one of the things about her that had drawn him, that candor.

If their night of comfort sex had left her pregnant, she'd have told him.

*When would she have had the chance?*

He'd left her still asleep, a hastily jotted note of explanation tucked under her pillow. Sleeping with her—hell, just being around her—had been dangerous. Matt's sudden death had come too closely on the heels of Cordero's vow of vengeance. Had Cordero had him killed as part of his vendetta against Luke?

It hadn't been out of the question. People he cared about automatically became targets.

He'd shipped out that morning for two years in Kaziristan, knowing she'd be hurt by his abandonment, hating every part of what he'd done. But it hadn't changed his determination to cut himself off from her and everyone he loved.

He'd meant his note to be a cold brush-off. He hadn't wanted her to try to contact him. If she'd found herself pregnant a few weeks later, he couldn't blame her for keeping that information to herself.

He almost missed the turn onto Abby's street. He slowed, made a quick right and reacquired Abby's silver Honda ahead. She pulled into a parking space in front of the building.

He took an empty spot nearby, hoping the building super wouldn't have the Mustang towed, and caught up with Abby on the sidewalk in front of the first apartment.

She jumped when he touched her arm. "Sorry," he said, wondering if he should just go ahead and ask her about Stevie's paternity. Would she tell him the truth?

Probably not, he realized. If she'd kept it a secret for three years, she wouldn't spill the beans just because a couple of gunmen had thrown her into Luke's life again.

He wouldn't push for now. It was the least he owed her.

"It's a mess," she warned him as she set Stevie down on the ground and unlocked the front door of her first-floor apartment.

She wasn't lying, he realized with dismay a few seconds later, taking in the torn sofa cushions, the books in scattered heaps where the searchers had pulled them from the bookshelf against the wall, the overturned coffee table with the shattered crystal box in shards on the hardwood floor.

"I didn't stop to clean up," she explained. "I needed to know if you knew what Matt might be hiding, so I just grabbed Stevie and headed out."

He picked up a couple of the books and put them back on the shelf. "Is the bedroom as bad?"

"The mattress is ripped open, but I can probably stuff most of the filling back inside and cover it with a sheet—"

"You can't stay here tonight, Abby. This is unlivable."

She squared her jaw. "I'll make it work."

"You don't have to make it work. Just grab some clothes, some toys for Little Bit and let's get the hell out of here. We can regroup and figure out what to do next once we're settled."

Her brow creased. "Settled where?"

He looked down at Stevie, who was toddling toward the ruins of the broken crystal box. Picking him up to keep him out of the sharp shards, he settled the wriggly little boy on one hip and met her troubled gaze.

"At my place, of course," he answered.

# Chapter Three

Abby stared at him, her mind racing through a checklist of reasons why moving herself and Stevie into Luke Cooper's house was a very bad idea. Beyond the tangled history between them, which was reason enough, she'd be putting Luke at risk at a time when he was supposed to be helping her find out what Matt had hidden and where. At least one of them needed to be able to get around San Diego without a team of thugs dogging every step.

"That's just not a good idea," she said.

"What's the alternative—book a room in a motel? Do you think motel security is worth a damn?" Luke shifted Stevie on his hip and met her gaze with a look of calm skepticism. Stevie turned his head toward her and gave her an almost identical look. She didn't know whether to laugh or to cry.

She couldn't argue with Luke's logic, however. She couldn't afford a few unexpected nights at a motel, and she'd probably be in even greater peril holed up with Stevie alone in a place where nobody knew or cared who they were.

"We don't have to complicate this," Luke said. "There's plenty of room for you and Little Bit there."

Her lips twitched at the nickname he'd apparently settled on for Stevie. "You don't owe us anything."

He started to say something, then narrowed his lips to a

tight line. After a moment, he said, "I can put you to work, if it'd make you feel better."

"Cooking and cleaning?"

He arched an eyebrow. "No. I've eaten your cooking."

She made a face, relieved by the lightness of Luke's tone. Better than the constant strain of the past hour. "I've gotten better. You might be surprised."

He smiled at her. "You always found ways to surprise me, Abs." His smile faded and he looked down at Stevie, who had rediscovered the hawk pendant and was twirling it around his sticky little fingers. "What do you say, Stevie? Wanna come stay with your uncle Luke for a few days?"

Abby struggled not to react to Luke's words, but guilt burned in her chest like acid. She should have told him the truth three years ago, when she realized she was carrying his child inside her. At the time, with Luke in a war-torn country continents away, settling on the easy lie hadn't seemed so wrong, especially given how abruptly and finally he'd left her bed—and life—after their night together.

But now that he was here in front of her, holding his son without even knowing it, she knew she'd been a coward. And Luke's bad behavior at the time didn't change the facts.

He had a son. He had a right to know.

When this was over, and everything had settled back down to normal, she'd tell him, she promised herself. She'd tell Luke he was Stevie's father, and then they'd figure out how to go on with their separate lives from there.

"Okay," she said finally. "For a couple of days."

He gave a quick nod, as if to affirm she was doing the right thing. "Can I help you pack?"

"Just keep Stevie occupied," she said, heading for the bedroom. Inside, she picked through the mess the intruders had left and found a few days' worth of clothes for her and for Stevie, which she packed in an empty gym bag she found tossed against the wall under the window. She added tooth-brushes, vitamins and a few other things Stevie would need into his diaper bag. His favorite book. The stuffed rabbit he didn't like to sleep without. Blinking back tears, she headed out to the living room.

She found Stevie sitting quietly in the wooden rocking chair near the corner, watching Luke sweep up the broken crystal box. Luke looked up as Abby entered, a faint frown on his face. "Matt gave you this, didn't he?"

She followed his gaze to the gold wildcat set into the cut crystal of the box's top. "For our wedding." Matt's nickname had been Wildcat, and at the time he'd given her the box, she'd thought the gesture wildly romantic, as if he were giving himself to her symbolically.

She hadn't realized that the box was almost all of himself he intended to give to her or any other woman. His first love was intrigue, and he'd have sacrificed anyone and anything for that beguiling temptress.

She took the piece of crystal from Luke's hand. It was warm, but only from the heat of Luke's fingers. She dropped it in the trash can by the kitchen nook and retrieved Stevie from the rocker, settling him on one hip. With the gym bag in her other hand, she looked back at Luke. "Let's go."

He caught up with her at the door, taking the bag from her hand. "He loved you, the best he knew how," he murmured as he opened the apartment door for her.

She knew he was right. Matt had loved her in his own way. She'd loved him, as well. For all his faults, he'd been a hard man not to love.

It just hadn't been enough.

THEY LEFT ABBY'S CAR at her apartment and took his Mustang, transferring Stevie's car seat before they left. As Luke navigated through light traffic on the way back to University

City, he found himself glancing in the rearview mirror now and then to check on the sleepy little boy, who'd fussed a bit when Abby had told him they were going on a trip.

"He's past his bedtime," Abby murmured. "He'll probably be asleep by the time we get there."

Luke looked at her. "You look pretty worn-out yourself."

Her lips curved. "Gee, thanks."

"I'll call my supervisor tonight and tell him I'm working from home the rest of the week." It was one of the perks of his job, directing his own schedule, for the most part. Now that the case in Rancho Santa Fe was over, he just had some paperwork to fill out and some loose ends to tie up, most of which he could do over the phone or by e-mail.

"What are you doing now?" she asked, stifling a yawn. "Jobwise, I mean."

"Security work. Protective detail, investigations. That sort of thing."

Her chuckle was low and warm, like cello music. He felt a rush of pure male heat flood his veins in response. "So, basically the same kind of work you did in the corps."

"Basically," he agreed, proud of how steady his voice emerged, despite the tremors going off low in his abdomen. He tried to concentrate on her question rather than his libido. "Compared to the corps, my job's a day at the beach. Sometimes literally." He grinned. "What about you? Where are you working these days?"

"I freelance with a couple of local school systems that don't have full-time speech therapists. A few nonprofits that need temporary translation services. Some private tutoring." She turned to look over her shoulder at Stevie. "I do some consulting work for Homeland Security, too. Linguistics stuff relating to wiretaps, that sort of thing. I'm looking to branch out, though. Bring in a little more money so we can afford a real house."

*MSI might be interested in her services,* he thought. For a moment, his first thought was to mention her to Dave Malkin to see if he could find her some more freelance work.

But he quickly quashed the notion. The last thing Abby and her son needed was to have Luke in their lives, even hanging around the periphery.

He was dangerous to know.

"Luke, what if we don't find what Matt took?" A tremble in Abby's voice belied her calm expression. "What if these people are wrong and he didn't take anything from them to begin with?"

"We're going to sort it out, I promise." He wasn't yet sure how, but the one thing he knew, as surely as he knew his own name, was that he wasn't going to let anyone hurt Abby or her son. He'd spent the past three years wishing he could have done things differently with Abby Chandler, and this was all the chance he could expect to make up for his mistakes.

He had no intention of letting her down this time.

He made the turn down his street and scanned the area, looking for anything that seemed out of place. He recognized all the vehicles parked within a block of his bungalow and didn't see any strange people walking the streets. He lowered the car window as he made a pass down his street once without stopping. He could hear the muted sound of music coming from within a couple of the houses, and here and there dogs barking, but nothing seemed out of sorts.

"Didn't we just pass your house?" Abby asked.

"Yeah. I wanted to drive around once, just to make sure everything's calm." He circled the block, moving neither too fast nor too slow, and kept his ears open. A block over, a beagle was baying frantically at something in the backyard of a small yellow stucco house located directly behind Luke's own backyard.

Might be a squirrel or an opossum driving him nuts.

Or not.

Luke pulled up the short drive to his garage and reached across to press the door opener. The whir of the door's machinery seemed deafening to his ears, though he knew from testing the security system that the sound of the garage door opening wasn't nearly as audible in the house.

But if someone had managed to bypass his silent alarm and made it inside his house, would the faint noise of the garage door opening give them warning that he was on his way?

"Is something wrong?" Abby asked softly.

He met her worried gaze, not surprised that she was able to read his body language so well. She'd always seemed to know what he was thinking and feeling more clearly than he had known himself. "I'm cautious," he admitted.

"Why don't you have a security system?"

"I do," he said with a smile. "It's a silent one. You tripped it, by the way."

"I'm an amateur. These people aren't."

He forced himself to smile. "So we'll be cautious. You and Stevie stay here in the garage. I'll lock the side door from the outside, so nobody should be able to get in. You'll have the door opener if you need to get out, and I'll leave the car key here with you." He removed the Mustang's ignition key from his key ring and handed it to her. "If you don't hear anything from me in ten minutes, get out of here and go to the nearest police station. Tell them everything you know."

He could tell from the look on her face that she had no intention of going to the police. But he wasn't going to sit out here in the garage all night arguing a hypothetical.

"Once I make sure the house is safe, I'll come back and get you." He got out of the car and closed the driver's door behind him, bending to look back in the open window. "We're going to figure this all out, Abs. I promise."

In her eyes he saw her desire to believe doing fierce battle with disillusionment. He wondered how much of that disillusionment was thanks to Matt's lies and how much was a product of his own grave mistakes.

He slipped out of the garage and locked the door safely behind him, walking the flagstone path to the house with care, knowing that one slip onto the pebbles below would alert anyone lurking inside his darkened house of his approach.

He eyed the side-door lock to see if it had been tampered with. Everything looked just as he'd left it. But he wasn't so egotistical as to believe there was no way an intruder could get past his security setup.

He closed his hand around the Glock at his belt and slipped it from the holster. Falling back on years of urban combat training, he entered the door fast and low, sweeping the kitchen for any signs of occupation.

It was empty.

He almost let his guard down at that point, listening to the familiar silence of the house. But he hadn't spent a decade in the Marine Corps just to forget the hard lessons.

He scanned the kitchen once more, looking for any signs of something out of place. The lack of disorder only amped up his tension. Because somewhere in his gut, he sensed he wasn't alone in the house.

Which meant whoever was waiting somewhere behind a door or around the corner was damned good at his job.

There were times to fight and times to regroup. Deciding which time was which was something he'd learned over almost ten years in uniform. Suicide missions were last-ditch options. Much smarter to beat a strategic retreat, then regroup and make a plan of attack from a more advantageous position.

Especially when you had a two-year-old boy and his mother waiting in the garage to be collateral damage.

He turned quietly and edged toward the back door. He

almost made it there before he heard a metallic click a few feet behind him.

"Major Luke Cooper, United States Marine Corps. Retired." The slick voice behind him ended with a soft clucking sound. "So young for a retiree. Battle fatigue?"

Luke started to turn around.

"I'd appreciate it if you lowered your gun," the man behind him added in what Luke guessed, from what Abby had told him, must be a Boston Brahmin accent.

"If you think I'm going to put my weapon on the floor and go down without a fight, you don't know much about the Marines," Luke said, his voice calmer than the roiling sensation in his gut would have suggested.

"I don't think either of us needs to use our weapons," the other man said, his tone slightly amused. "In fact, I think we probably want the same thing, don't we?"

Luke lowered his Glock to his side but didn't holster it. He turned around to find the man Abby had described from her earlier encounter—tall, muscular, dressed in black from head to toe. The ski mask fit him snugly, hiding all but a circle of pale skin around his sharp blue eyes and two thin, hard lips. He held a nasty-looking Colt M1991 in his left hand.

"I suppose we want the same thing," Luke agreed, "but I doubt we'll agree on what to do with it."

The thin lips curved into a humorless smile. "Well, I guess we'll have to deal with that when the time comes. Meanwhile, Mrs. Chandler has told you what my employer wants."

"Actually, she doesn't seem very certain what it is we're looking for," Luke countered, wondering how many other people were hiding in his house. One more? Two? Three? He'd feel a lot more confident about what he needed to do next if he had some way of knowing what he was up against.

"Captain Chandler took something from my employer. He wants it back."

"Something? That's a little vague."

"You'll know it if you find it."

"Also vague." Luke cocked his head. "Your employer must not think very much of you if he couldn't even tell you what you're threatening women and children to find."

The other man drew a swift breath through his nose, sucking the black knit up tighter against his face. His eyes flashed with hate, but when he spoke, it was in the same slightly bemused tone he'd used all along. "You served with Captain Chandler. You were close friends."

"Look who knows how to use Google."

The masked man smiled again. "You served side by side with the captain in Afghanistan four years ago, and again with him in Sanselmo shortly before he died."

"What did you do, memorize my service jacket?" Luke asked, feigning boredom, although the intruder's breadth of knowledge about his time in the Marines suggested he had some pretty well-connected sources, probably in the government.

Which meant they were up against an even tougher enemy than he'd anticipated.

The intruder's smile grew ugly as he saw through Luke's mask of indifference. "You see, I wasn't bluffing when I told Mrs. Chandler she really had no choice but to help us find what we're looking for."

"She didn't think you were."

"We were wondering who she'd run to for help." There was a hint of innuendo in the man's tone that made Luke's skin crawl. "You see, we knew she'd go to the person most likely to know what her husband had been hiding from her."

"But you didn't know who that was?"

"We do now." The masked man chuckled. "Isn't technology wonderful? A phone call, a text message, and in mere moments, almost everything you need to know is at your fingertips."

"You should be in a commercial." Luke made a show of looking around the spotless kitchen. "Should I feel insulted that you didn't trash my place the way you did Abby's?"

"You haven't seen the rest of the house."

Luke arched one eyebrow. "Say, did you find a dark green sock anywhere? I've been looking for it for weeks."

The man's smile faded. "Seven days, Major Cooper. Mrs. Chandler clearly believes you can help her find what we're looking for. If you can, I suggest you do."

"Or what? You'll hurt a two-year-old?" Luke sneered. "What a fulfilling job you have."

The masked man took a swift step forward. Luke's gun hand twitched upward.

A second man in a black mask stepped around the corner into the kitchen and put a restraining hand on the other man's arm. He murmured something Luke couldn't quite make out.

The man with the Brahmin accent visibly took himself under control. "Seven days."

"Got it. Now get out of my house."

The second man—African-American, Luke noted, just as Abby had described—nodded toward the back of the house. He went around the corner and out of sight.

The other man stayed where he was, staring Luke down. Luke didn't drop his gaze, more than happy to wait him out.

"Don't let me down," the man said. Then he turned as well, disappearing around the corner on silent feet.

Luke stayed where he was, knowing that trying to stop them was a fool's game that wouldn't end well. He tightened his grip on the Glock, waiting for the sound of a window opening in the back of the house.

It came, softer than he'd expected. They'd probably greased

the window first to cut down on the creaks. He didn't hear it close at all, but after a couple of minutes, he decided it was safe to check the rest of the house.

The man in the mask hadn't been lying. Both bedrooms, both bathrooms and the living room had been trashed in a fast but thorough search. He suspected they'd searched the kitchen as well, though they'd clearly taken more care to hide their tracks there, apparently knowing from their earlier reconnaissance that he customarily entered through the side door. Easier to get the upper hand if they didn't leave a calling card for him to discover the second he walked through the door.

He was surprised they hadn't tried the garage.

Or had they?

Unease squirming in his belly, he raced to the garage, unlocked the door and let himself in. The place was just as he'd left it, no sign of a struggle or anything out of place. They'd probably checked here first, he realized, and, as they had with the kitchen, left it as they'd found it in order to cover their tracks.

Inside the car, Abby had shifted to the driver's side, her pale face staring back at him through the Mustang's open window.

"Is it safe?" she asked softly.

He thought about the ease with which Abby had broken into his house earlier. It was probably ten times easier for the intruders he'd just encountered in his kitchen. And they'd been able to disable the silent alarm before it sent him a warning. Had they had access to his personal files at MSI? What else might they know about him and his life in San Diego?

"No," he answered Abby's question firmly, reaching into the car to unlatch the trunk. He checked the trunk to make sure the duffel bag he kept stashed there for emergency travel was still in place. It was, and a cursory check of the contents reassured him that he had enough extra clothes and supplies inside to get him through the next few days.

Abby had gotten out of the car and come around to stand beside him, her gaze flickering down to the travel bag. "We're not staying here tonight, are we?"

He shook his head. "No, we're not."

"What happened?"

He told her about the intruders, keeping it short and sweet. But even his sanitized account was enough to reignite the terror that had finally started to fade from her blue eyes. She bit her lip and looked back into the car at Stevie, who was sleeping peacefully in his car seat.

Her chin came up, and when she spoke, there was not a hint of shakiness in her voice. "Where are we going?"

Until that moment, he hadn't thought that far ahead. But clearly, staying in San Diego would only subject them to more surprise visits from their tormentors. Luke wasn't foolish enough to assume their bark was worse than their bite; nobody played such aggressive mind games unless they were pretty damned sure they had the goods to back up their threats. Whoever their employer was, he had high-powered connections and, Luke assumed, enough firepower to do what he threatened.

Luke might be a well-trained retired Marine who could still hold his own in a fight, but going up against that kind of enemy alone was stupid. He needed backup and he needed to change the playing field to give himself the advantage. And there was only one place he could think of where he'd have the upper hand.

"Right now," he answered Abby, "we're going to find a cheap motel where they'll take cash and ask no questions."

"And after that?"

He smiled genuinely for the first time in a long time. "Ever been to Alabama?"

# Chapter Four

"If they know all about you, won't they be staking out your family?" Abby broke the tense silence that had hovered between them for almost three hours. Interstate signs signaled that they were nearing the outskirts of Yuma, Arizona. The drive east had taken longer than it should've, thanks to Luke's wandering tour of eastern San Diego before they'd hit I-8 near El Cajon.

The dashboard clock inched toward 11:00 p.m.

"I haven't been back to Alabama in almost ten years," Luke answered flatly. "They know that."

"That long?" She looked up in surprise. He'd always spoken lovingly of his big, boisterous family in Gossamer Ridge. For Abby, an only child whose parents had passed away in a car crash when she was eighteen, Luke's stories of his wonderful, crazy family had always evoked a sense of envy.

"It's complicated."

She tamped down an acid rush of bitterness. The job, of course. Military intel—the secrets, the lies, the constant danger all took a toll. Marriages crumbled, friends became enemies, families self-destructed.

She glanced at Stevie, sound asleep in his car seat. He was still young enough that car travel was a surefire sleep aid. At least he could sleep in peace tonight. She'd do anything to spare him even a second of fear or concern.

"We're stopping in Yuma for the night," Luke said. She saw his gaze fixed on the rearview mirror. Did he see Stevie in the reflection,? Could he see how Stevie's square jaw was a carbon copy of his own??

For his first year, Stevie had looked just like her, saving her from awkward questions and convoluted explanations about his origins. But now that she saw glimpses of Luke in her son—the darkening gray eyes, his lopsided smile—she was painfully aware of how selfish she'd been to keep father and son apart just to avoid complications.

Maybe Luke hadn't wanted her enough to stick around. But that didn't mean he wouldn't want to know their son.

"You haven't contacted anyone since we left my house, have you?" Luke asked. "Maybe when we stopped at the ATM?"

"No." His sudden tension made her stomach hurt. "Why?"

His gaze darted to the rearview mirror. "That car a quarter mile back's been with us for the last few miles. I slow down, speed up, no matter. He stays the same distance away."

Over her shoulder, all she saw was a blur of lights. But she trusted him. "What do we do?"

"Take this exit and see what happens." Luke whipped the Mustang into a narrow gap between a truck and a sedan just in time to take a quick right onto the off-ramp.

"Did it work?" Abby's heart raced from the daredevil move.

"Can't tell yet." At the bottom of the off-ramp, Luke went right and pulled into a well-lit gas station nearby. He cut the engine by one of the pumps, keeping his eyes on the exit ramp. "You pump the gas." He pulled his wallet from his jacket pocket and handed it to her.

Tamping down fear, Abby took money from the wallet and headed off to prepay the cashier. When she returned, she found Luke rummaging through the trunk.

"Did they follow us?" She unscrewed the cover of the Mustang's gas tank.

"Not sure." He closed the trunk. In his left hand, he held a small gray device with red lights at the top. One light was lit up. He showed it to her. "See that light? There's a GPS tracking device within a twenty-five-foot radius."

There were no other cars at the gas station, and the road was at least forty feet away. "Does your car have GPS?"

He shook his head. "I never wanted it used against me. Do you have a GPS tag on any of Stevie's stuff?"

"I don't let him out of my sight except to take him to Mrs. Tamburello's while I'm working." She returned the gas nozzle to the pump, her mind racing. "You know, I don't know how long those men were in my apartment—"

Luke opened the driver's door of the Mustang and shoved back the driver's seat. Hearing Stevie's soft whimper, she raced around to the passenger door. "What are you doing?" she demanded, glaring at Luke across the backseat.

Luke's expression of horror was almost comical. "God, I'm sorry—I wasn't—" He laid his hand on Stevie's head, stroking his damp curls. "Sorry about wakin' you up there, Little Bit."

Stevie's snuffling subsided. "Firsty."

"You're thirsty, huh?" He glanced at Abby.

"I'll get him an apple juice." She ran to the food mart, grabbed an apple juice from one of the coolers and added it to the gas purchase. Back at the car, Luke stood by the driver's side door, Stevie cradled in his arms. Abby faltered, her heart stuttering at the sight of Luke's big, muscular arms wrapped around their son.

She was going to have to tell him the truth. Soon.

Luke's gaze locked with hers as she reached the Mustang. He held up a black device a little smaller than a credit card. "Found it inside Mr. Hoppy." He nodded toward the small animatronic stuffed rabbit sitting on the roof of the car, its ears still wiggling and nose twitching. "Inside the pouch where the batteries are. I guess they put it there when they trashed your house."

Her heart lurched. "So they know where we are."

He nodded. "No wonder they didn't risk a wreck to follow us off the interstate. They can pick us up wherever we go."

"Throw it away!" The sensation of being watched made her skin crawl.

Luke shook his head. "I have a better idea."

THE BUDGET ARMS MOTEL was the sort of nondescript, vaguely shabby motel a motorist could find near almost any major interstate exit. Walk-ins were welcome if there were vacancies, and some of the places didn't even require identification as long as you could pay cash up front for the room. The only amenities would be basic cable and local phone service, if that.

Luke had stayed in worse places.

Abby, apparently, had not, judging by the look of horror on her face when Luke pulled into the motel parking lot.

"This is your better idea?"

"Wait here," he said, parking in front of the motel office. As Abby started to protest, he leaned toward her, cupping her chin in his palm. "Trust me, Abs. I know what I'm doing."

He could see the struggle in her blue-eyed gaze, but her expression finally cleared and she gave a little nod.

He handed her the keys before he got out. "Any sign of trouble and you get the hell out of here, understand me? Just go. I've got the tracker, so they can't find you that way."

She nodded again, worry flooding back into her eyes.

He pocketed the GPS tracker as he got out of the Mustang and headed up the uneven concrete walk to the office. Inside he found a dark-haired man reading a bodybuilding magazine. He looked up with a hint of annoyance as Luke entered.

"I need a room for a couple of nights." Luke pulled his wallet from his jacket pocket.

The desk clerk handed him a register. "Sign here."

Luke knew better than to sign his own name. The people following him would smell that kind of trap a mile away. But for his purposes, he needed to pick a name that could, with a little research, be connected to him. He settled on Cal Trimble, the name of his old drill sergeant at Parris Island. Obscure, but not so obscure that people with resources couldn't connect it to him with a little effort.

It served his purposes for the people who were following them to think they'd finally found them.

Paying the fee for two nights, he pocketed the room key the clerk handed him and headed back outside to a pay phone attached to the office facade. He put coins into the slot to make a call he knew might end up being traced, as well. That was okay, too. It wasn't as if he didn't make calls to his family now and then.

His sister answered, her voice groggy. "Yeah?"

"Hey, Hannah, it's Luke."

"Hey, stranger." A smile tinted her sleepy voice, and he heard a low-pitched murmur on the other end of the line. "It's Luke," he heard Hannah say in response.

"I need to speak to your husband," Luke said.

"You need to speak to Riley?" Hannah sounded puzzled. Luke couldn't blame her; he'd yet to meet her husband, despite the fact that she'd been married to the former Wyoming cop for over a year. A couple of months earlier, she'd given birth to her first child, a little boy they'd named Cody.

He missed her like hell. He'd stayed away from home far too long, let too many milestones go unwitnessed. Hannah's wedding. Jake's whirlwind romance with his pretty wife,

Mariah. Sam's return to Gossamer Ridge after years away, and his recent marriage. His niece Cissy's graduation.

He'd missed all of it because going home had seemed too big a risk. But wasn't what he was doing now even more dangerous? Cordero or the black-clad thugs—what was the difference?

Was he doing the wrong thing again?

"Is something wrong?" Hannah asked.

He shook off his doubts. He needed help. He knew he could count on his family for backup. End of story. "Let me talk to Riley and then he can explain."

"Okay." He heard the reluctance in his sister's voice as she passed the phone to her husband.

"Hi, Luke." Riley Patterson's voice was a low rumble tinged with a Wyoming twang. "Something up?"

A lot was up, but he didn't have time to do anything but get to the point. "Do your parents still live in Yuma?"

"HAVE YOU EVEN met them before?" Abby resisted the urge to look out the window of the motel. She was pretty sure that whoever had been following them on I-8 had found them by now. Luke had assured her more than once that letting the bad guys find them was all part of his plan.

She wished she could feel quite so confident.

"No, I haven't met them. I haven't even met Riley."

She looked away from the closed curtains. "You haven't met your brother-in-law? Not even at the wedding?"

A flicker of pain crossed Luke's face before his features settled into a carefully neutral expression. "I told you, I haven't been home in ten years."

Abby shook her head and turned back toward the window. Luke had no idea how lucky he was to have a big family to go home to. "What makes you sure you can trust him?"

"Hannah trusts him. She's always been a good judge

of character. A lot better than any of her hardheaded brothers."

She smiled a little at the confidence in his voice. For a guy who'd been avoiding home for so long, he clearly loved his family dearly. What in his secret past could have kept him away from them for ten years?

Outside the motel room, a new sound interrupted the faint drone of traffic on the interstate—the low-pitched purr of a car engine. The sound died too suddenly for a passing car. Someone had entered the motel parking lot and shut off the engine. Was it the people they were waiting for?

Abby looked at Luke, her pulse quickening. His expression didn't change as he crossed calmly to the tiny dressing room vanity and picked up the scuffed plastic ice bucket.

"Showtime," he said, nodding toward the door near the back of the room. He'd already made quick work of the simple locks separating their room from the empty one next door. He'd stashed their bags and Stevie's car seat by the front door of the adjoining suite, ready for their quick getaway.

Luke detoured to the bed and picked up Stevie. Abby held her breath, even though she knew Stevie was next to impossible to wake once he was dead asleep. He grumbled softly but didn't awaken, and Abby exhaled.

Exchanging a quick look with her, Luke tucked Stevie close and joined her at the door to the adjoining room.

"What if they jump you outside?" Abby paused with her hand on the doorknob, fear freezing her insides.

"They won't go after me when I have Stevie. These people may be ruthless, but they don't really want to hurt a kid."

She reached out to stroke her son's silky hair. Fear crystallized in the pit of her belly. "You hope."

"I think." His expression softened, and he started to lift the hand holding the ice bucket. He let it drop again, a little wrinkle of frustration forming between his eyes.

Abby wondered what that aborted gesture meant. Had he been planning to touch her? She was alarmed by how much she craved his touch right now. How gladly she'd have walked into his arms had he spread them open to welcome her.

"I'll protect him with my life, Abs. Nobody's going to hurt him on my watch."

Nobody was better prepared to follow through on the promise he'd just made. But she'd seen their pursuers in action. They were equally skilled, and unlike Luke, they had plenty of resources backing them up.

"I know you're afraid," Luke added. "But this is our best chance to go to ground awhile to get them off our trail."

She met his steady gaze, struggling to draw strength from his confidence. "I'll be waiting for your knock."

He smiled briefly as she opened the door and entered the adjoining room. As she locked the door behind her, she heard Luke doing the same thing to the door on their side.

The people after them were as capable of picking locks as Luke—if they'd even bother with stealth. But two locked doors would at least give her a head start on escaping.

She resisted the urge to watch through the narrow gap in the curtains, not wanting to alert their pursuers to her presence in the second room. Instead, she sat on the edge of the bed in the dark, counting every frantic heartbeat to pass the time while she waited for Luke's signal.

LUKE STAYED CLOSE to the motel façade, keeping to the shadows, not because he thought that such a maneuver would help him evade detection but because he knew it wouldn't. He was dealing with pros who apparently knew a lot about his background. If he didn't at least try to avoid being seen, they'd know he was setting a trap.

His plan, long shot that it was, depended on the enemy believing he didn't have a plan.

Against his shoulder, Stevie stirred as the cold November air slid under the blanket tucked around him. "Mama?"

"Shh," Luke murmured, tucking him closer. Knowing the little boy's sleepy whimpers would carry in the crisp night breeze, Luke made a show of trying to quiet him, but he didn't really mind if anyone heard. Trying to walk a restless child into falling back to sleep created a pretty good reason for him to be outside the room at this time of night. Fortunately, Stevie settled right back to sleep.

He took his time walking to the ice machine near the motel office, keeping his eyes peeled for any sign of movement. He caught the flicker of light coming from inside a dark sedan parked near the end of the parking lot, so faint that almost anyone else might assume he'd just imagined it. But in a glance, Luke assured himself that the parked vehicle was the one that had been following them for miles.

Reaching the corner, he turned, heading down the narrow breezeway to where the ice machine and a couple of drink vending machines filled a small alcove hidden from view of the parking lot. But instead of turning into the alcove, he continued on past the ice machine to the rear of the motel.

A narrow dirt alley ran behind the building, an access point for trash retrieval from the large Dumpster located behind the front office. Luke headed quickly down the alley, rounded the office and edged his way along the side of the building until he had a decent view of the parking lot from the shadows.

He saw a dark figure glide silently across the parking lot and disappear into the gloom under the eaves of the brick building, heading in the direction of Luke's motel room.

*Bold bastards,* he thought.

The black-clad man looked shorter and stockier than the two who'd invaded Luke's house earlier that evening. He'd been right. The people who were after what Matt stole had resources and, apparently, plenty of willing operatives.

This almost had to be about Voices for Villages and Janis Meeks. Had Matt found evidence tying Barton Reid to the arms-for-drugs deals? It was an open secret in foreign policy circles that Reid had a philosophical affinity with *El Cambio* and their political aims. Had Matt found some sort of evidence to prove that one of the State Department's top men put his personal leanings over the stated foreign policy of his own government to the point of arming narco-terrorists?

If these men really were acting as Barton Reid's personal army, there were probably few lines they wouldn't cross to get rid of that kind of damning evidence.

Luke glanced at the car parked at the end of the lot. It appeared to be empty. But was it? He knew there had to be at least two operatives tailing them; anything less was bad procedure. Could there be three or more? Possibly, but Luke doubted it. On an operation like this, stealth was key, so you went with as few operatives as possible. Two well-trained men would be enough to handle Luke, a female civilian and a toddler, especially if they had the element of surprise.

He slid deeper into the shadows, back toward the alley. Keeping close to the sheltering bulk of the Dumpster, he looked down the narrow lane, praying Riley had come through for him.

There. The faint gleam of a streetlamp bounced off the fender of a car parked at the street end of the alley. Light blue sedan, just as Riley had promised.

Everything was set. Now he just had to locate the two operatives who'd been following him so he'd know which of their plans to set into motion.

Luke crept toward the breezeway, pausing at the corner when he heard soft footsteps, close enough so that his heart skipped a beat. He waited as the steps paused. Checking the alcove to see where Luke had disappeared to?

If he could take this operative out of commission, he might

have an upper hand with the one he'd seen heading for the motel room. But he couldn't exactly fight with a two-year-old on his shoulder. And while the seconds ticked away, Abby was waiting in a hotel room for his signal, in escalating danger.

The footsteps resumed, moving toward him. He padded silently back toward the edge of the building, where shadows from the bare branches of a large cottonwood tree gave him extra cover. He ducked behind the cottonwood and peered toward the breezeway exit, where a man dressed in black crept into the alley, his movements deliberate and controlled.

This was a fourth operative, Luke realized—neither the stocky man from the parking lot nor one of the two men who'd trashed his house. This man was tall and whipcord-lean.

And he was looking straight at Luke.

# Chapter Five

Stevie stirred against Luke's neck, and for a second, all the air froze in Luke's lungs. *Please, Little Bit, please don't wake up. Hang on just a little longer.*

He stayed perfectly still, hoping the shadows hid them from view. The longer the man in black stood there, staring, the more certain Luke was that he and Stevie had been spotted.

The man scanned the alley for movement. Luke's chest began to burn from holding his breath. Finally, the operative ducked back into the breezeway, disappearing from sight.

Luke darted down the alley toward the back of the motel building, looking for the *X* he'd painted with toothpaste on the bathroom window of the adjoining room. Though small, the window was big enough for Abby to crawl through. Their bags would also go through the window; he'd checked beforehand, in case a back-door exit became necessary.

Spotting flashes of light coming from within the motel room he'd rented earlier, Luke made up his mind. A rear exit was necessary. He rapped softly on the bathroom window, hoping the sound was loud enough for Abby to hear him without the men next door being alerted.

Time crept while he waited for Abby to respond. He was on the verge of knocking again when the window creaked open and Abby's heart-shaped face appeared in the window.

"I can hear them moving around next door," she whispered.

"I know. Time for plan B. Go get the bags."

"Already did." She dropped from sight briefly and popped back into view with his soft-sided duffel, passing it through the window to him. As quietly as possible, she handed the other two bags through the window, her expression growing more and more strained each time.

"They're picking the locks to the adjoining room," she said as she bent to grab something else.

"Leave it. Crawl through now!" he ordered urgently.

"I can't—it's Stevie's car seat." She hauled the folded seat over the windowsill and let it drop into Luke's free arm. He grabbed it and lowered it to the ground, rising to help Abby out of the room. But she was already through the window, tumbling down awkwardly and hitting with a bone-jarring thud.

She grunted with pain, and Luke's stomach gave a sickening lurch. "Are you hurt?" he whispered, bending to check on her.

She shook off his hand. "I'm fine. I heard the adjoining door opening and figured I'd get out while I could. Let's go!"

He handed Stevie to her. "There's a car parked at the end of the alley. Go! Riley's dad is waiting. I'll get the bags."

She looked reluctant but started running, holding Stevie pressed close to her chest. Luke grabbed their bags, along with Stevie's car seat, hooking them together with the longer handle of his duffel bag. It was an awkward, heavy load, but he'd carried heavier in worse conditions.

Trying to ignore the sounds coming through the open window behind him, he set off after Abby, catching up as they neared the parked sedan. The back door of the car opened, but no light emerged from the interior.

Luke skidded to a stop, grabbing Abby's arm. Why hadn't the dome light come on? Was it a trap?

A moment later, the front driver's window lowered, and the lean, craggy face of a man in his sixties appeared through the opening. "You folks gettin' in or not?" he asked, his blue eyes sharp with urgency.

Luke nudged Abby into the backseat and handed her Stevie's car seat. As she started buckling Stevie in, Luke raced around to enter the passenger side, quickly turning to look down the alley toward the motel. He spotted a black-masked head sticking out of the open window Abby had just come through.

He turned to the gray-haired man at the wheel. "Go. Now."

The man cranked the engine, slammed the car into gear and shot out of the alley, taking a quick turn down the next street. He drove with silent intensity for the next ten minutes, darting the car down side streets and through narrow alleys until they finally cut through a large intersection as the light was turning yellow and headed up the on-ramp to I-8.

Luke turned around to look at Abby, who stared back at him with wide, scared eyes. Strapped snugly into the car seat next to her, Stevie was sound asleep. He'd never really awakened through the entire ordeal.

He reached over the seat and grabbed Abby's hand, giving it a quick squeeze. She squeezed back, and for a second, he felt as if all the years between them disappeared, and they were back in San Diego, with no secrets or betrayals between them.

They'd been the best of friends, once. Soul mates, even. If things had been different...

He let go, a ripping sensation clawing at his heart, and faced forward, gazing ahead at the lights of the interstate.

Things weren't different. Things were exactly the same as the night he'd walked out of her bedroom and her life.

He couldn't afford to lose sight of that fact.

Up on the interstate, the sedan dropped to a reasonable rate of speed. The gray-haired man in the driver's seat visibly relaxed and shot Luke a look of pure satisfaction. He spoke with an accent as dry and sprawling as the plains of Wyoming. "Nice to meet you finally, Luke Cooper. I'm Jim Patterson. I'd say we just had ourselves one hell of a welcome to the family."

THE PATTERSONS LIVED in a pretty, three-bedroom adobe-style house in the middle of a small neighborhood east of downtown Yuma. Jim Patterson parked the sedan next to a large Ford Bronco and cut the engine. "Patterson Ranch Southwest," he said with a wry smile. "You folks hungry? If I know Rita, she's got something warmin' up in the oven." He patted his flat belly. "She swears she's gonna fatten me up in my old age. I'm a little afraid to ask her what for."

Abby chuckled, the sound alien to her ears after the past few tense hours. She caught Luke's eye as they exited the car.

He smiled encouragingly. "Need me to get Little Bit?"

She shook her head and bent to retrieve Stevie from his car seat. He whined a little at being disturbed but settled down quickly, cuddling into her shoulder.

"When Riley was that size, he could sleep through a blizzard," Jim Patterson said. "What's his name?"

"Stevie. Stephen Chandler." She almost stumbled over the last name, guilt slicing into her gut like a knife. "I can't tell you how much I appreciate your taking us in like this."

Jim smiled. "Luke here is family. And if you're under his protection, that makes you family, too."

The urge to cry hit her like a physical blow. The handful

of people she still considered her family seemed so far away right now, farther than just the few hundred miles between here and her hometown of Texarkana. She struggled against tears, concentrating instead on the solid feel of Stevie's sleeping body tucked against her chest. His breath warmed the side of her neck, a potent reminder of what was at stake.

She would endure anything to protect her son. He was her family now. Maybe all the family she'd ever have again.

Jim had been right; the warm, fragrant scent of baking bread filled the air inside the house when they entered. A tall, rawboned woman emerged from the back of the house, smiling her welcome. She was in her early sixties, with an unruly thatch of rusty-red hair only moderately sprinkled with gray. She wore a pair of well-worn jeans paired incongruously with a bright green ruffled blouse.

The adoring gaze Jim Patterson sent her way made Abby's chest ache. "Told you we'd find her cookin'," he said with an affectionate grin. "I swear, woman, you're tryin' to kill me off for my fortune."

Rita's laugh was as bold and big as she was. "Hush up, old man, before you scare off the company. I'm Rita." Her warm, welcoming gaze settled on Stevie, and her green eyes softened, along with her voice. "What a little sweetie!"

"This is Stevie," Abby replied.

"I made up a bed for the two of you right in here. Let's get him settled down, how about it?" Rita led Abby into a short hallway and opened the first door on the right. "We just turned this room into a nursery for our new grandson," she said with a beaming grin.

The nursery was small, painted with blue and white stripes, and furnished with a crib and a twin-size bed. Abby laid Stevie in the crib under a small blue-and-white patchwork quilt. He was restless for a second, then settled down to sleep again.

"Luke's sister is married to our son Riley, you know," Rita whispered, picking up a photograph sitting on the night-stand by the bed. "They just had a little boy. Cody James Patterson."

Abby took the photo Rita handed her. It was a candid snap-shot of a woman with shoulder-length brown hair and bright green eyes, her face pale and tired but her smile so bright it seemed to light up the entire photo. She lay in a hospital bed, a tiny, red-faced baby tucked against her shoulder, screaming his newborn fury at being pulled from the warm, quiet cocoon that had kept him safe for nine long months.

At the woman's side, gazing not at the camera but at his wife, sat a rangy, ruggedly handsome man with sun-bronzed skin and rust-brown hair. The adoration in his eyes brought stinging tears to Abby's eyes.

She'd given birth to Stevie alone, with a nurse and her obstetrician to witness his entry into the world. Matt was dead and Luke somewhere across the globe, neither the nomi-nal father nor the biological one there to share the precious moment of Stevie's first wailing breath.

Had Luke known about his son, had he not been on active duty halfway across the world, would he have been there with her for Stevie's birth?

She had a sinking feeling she already knew the answer.

"They're a beautiful family," she said aloud to Rita.

Rita's green eyes were warm with sympathy. "I take it you're not with Stevie's father anymore?"

"My husband died in a car accident before Stevie was born."

"I'm sorry. That must have made your pregnancy such a difficult time."

"In some ways," she agreed, not wanting to talk about Matt or the past. "Mrs. Patterson, thank you so much for taking us in. I don't know how much you know about what's happening—"

"Only what Luke told Jim over the phone. You have no idea what these people are looking for?"

Abby shook her head. "Matt didn't tell me much about his work. I guess he couldn't, legally."

"I think Luke's idea to come here was sound, but I don't know if you should stay here very long. If these people are as ruthless as Luke seems to think, they'll eventually figure out he made a call to a man whose folks live right here in Yuma. We'd better figure out a way to get you safely out of Arizona and headed wherever it is you're going."

"That's just what I was telling Jim," Luke said from the bedroom doorway.

Abby locked gazes with him, alarmed by how eagerly her heart leaped at the sight of him. He'd been out of her sight for a matter of a few minutes, and she felt as excited as if he'd just returned from a long tour of duty.

*Don't do this, Abby. Don't fall back into this trap. It won't end well. It can't.*

Luke nodded his head toward the hallway, silently suggesting they take the conversation elsewhere. Abby gave the quilt around Stevie one more tug and a pat, then followed Rita out of the bedroom.

They ended up in the cozy living room, settled around a coffee table where Jim had set a tray of sticky buns and a large pot of coffee. Luke poured a cup for Abby, adding a teaspoon of sugar and a splash of creamer, just the way she liked it.

Their fingers touched as he passed the mug to her, making her hand tremble so much that she almost spilled the coffee. She set the mug down on a coaster quickly, dragging her gaze from Luke's before her out-of-control emotions betrayed her further.

"They don't have another tracker on us anywhere," Luke

said. "I checked with the scanner as soon as we were out of the alley. It's not likely they'll figure out where we've gone for the next little while. But they'll learn I made a phone call from the public phone at the motel, and if we're right about how connected these people are, they'll trace the call I made to Riley."

"If they do any snooping into Riley's background, they'll find us," Jim Patterson added. He looked at his wife, his bright blue eyes apologetic. "Rita, hon, we might be gettin' a visit sooner or later."

Abby's heart sank. "Oh, my God. They will come here, won't they? They'll want to know if you have any idea where we went."

Rita reached across to pat Abby's hand. "Jim and I figured out pretty quick what we were getting ourselves into, as soon as Luke called us. We're not afraid of a little trouble."

Abby didn't think Rita had any idea what kind of trouble might come calling. She turned to Luke. "We need to get out of here. Now. Before they connect us to the Pattersons."

"We don't have a car anymore," Luke pointed out. She could see from the worry in his eyes that he wasn't blind to the difficulties they were bringing down on Jim and Rita Patterson, but the grim set of his jaw suggested that he'd made peace with the consequences, at least for the moment.

How did he do it? Was it something the Marine Corps had taught him, how to live with the imperfect outcomes inherent in the sort of lives they led?

Abby couldn't be quite so sanguine. The thought of those two black-clad thugs making a visit to Jim and Rita because of something Abby had done— "There has to be a way to keep those creeps from finding out the Pattersons helped us."

"It's too late for that, hon," Rita said. "What's done is done."

Abby turned desperately to Luke. "What if they get rough with them? You saw those men."

"They're pros, Abs. And pros don't start breaking fingers when a little deceit will do."

"If they come to question us, they'll pretend to be law enforcement. FBI or something like that," Jim said.

"That does make sense," Rita agreed.

"It'll make it much easier for them to believe us when we tell them where the two of you were headed when you left here," Jim added with a grin. "We're law-abiding folks. We wouldn't dream of gettin' crossways with the law. Hell, I might even draw 'em a map."

Abby slanted a look at Luke. "A map to where?"

"They're going to tell whoever asks that they sent us up to Wyoming to stay with some friends of theirs up there. The Garrisons—Joe Garrison is a cop up there. Riley used to work with him."

"But since we're not going to Wyoming—"

"They won't find us. But if anyone asks the Pattersons where we went, that's what they'll say."

"I'm going to call Joe first thing in the morning to let him know he might be hearing from some folks claiming to be from the government," Jim added. "And that if he's asked, you folks were supposed to come for a visit but never showed up."

Rita looked admiringly at her husband. "You're a clever old fox, aren't you?"

Abby was overwhelmed by the eagerness of these two complete strangers to put themselves on the line to help her and Stevie.

"Meanwhile," Jim added, "I'd say we could all use a little shut-eye."

"Abby, I figured you'd want to stay in the room with Stevie. Luke, you can take the other guest room."

"Actually, I think I'd like to set up out here on the sofa, if that's okay," Luke suggested, glancing at Abby.

He intended to play security guard all night, Abby realized. Out here in the living room, he'd have a better shot at defending the main entrances, just in case they didn't shake their pursuers as easily as they'd thought.

Rita and Jim exchanged a look. Rita got up from her chair. "I'll get you a blanket and some pillows."

Luke thanked her and rose himself. "Jim, I really don't know how to thank you."

"Your sister's put me in your whole family's debt," Jim answered, his usually cheerful expression going deadly serious. "When Riley's first wife died, it felt like we lost our boy with her. Hannah's given him back to us. We love her like our own, and as far as I'm concerned, all you Coopers are family, too. So no thanks are necessary." Jim held out his hand.

Luke shook it firmly, his expression equally sober. But Abby could see the pain lining his eyes and wondered, yet again, just why he'd exiled himself so completely from the family he so clearly loved.

She had the opportunity to broach the subject a little later, when Luke followed her into the nursery to make sure she had everything she needed for the night.

"The Pattersons are good people," she murmured as he bent briefly over the crib to check on Stevie.

He turned his head to look at her. "Yeah."

"They sure love your sister."

"She's easy to love." Though he smiled, Abby heard a bleak note in his voice.

"Why haven't you been home in ten years?" she asked, deciding bluntness was the best approach.

Luke remained silent so long that Abby began to wonder if he planned to respond at all. When he finally spoke, it was the same nonanswer he'd given her before. "I told you, it's complicated."

She was inclined to press him for a better answer, but before she could speak, he asked a question of his own. "Did you stay in San Diego when you left base housing? Or did you return later?"

She wasn't sure why he was asking that question. Did he want her to admit that she'd stuck around San Diego the whole time, waiting for his return? She had stayed, but not out of any expectations where Luke was concerned. Matt had already taught her that pinning her hopes and dreams on an intelligence officer was a gamble she didn't have the heart for any longer. Luke hadn't even promised, in the letter he'd left on her pillow, to be in touch. It hadn't taken her long to realize she couldn't expect to hear from him again.

With a tiny life growing inside her, she had no longer allowed herself the luxury of false hope.

"I stayed in San Diego. My friends were there. My job prospects."

"Your doctor."

She nodded, her gaze sliding past him to look at her sleeping son. "That was also a consideration."

"I know I'd have been hard to track down, if you'd tried. But I wonder—" He stopped, his mouth pressing to a thin line. "I guess I don't really have to wonder, do I?"

She saw guilt in his eyes, darkening them to loamy gray-green. He regretted the bad goodbye, clearly. Despite her own sense of betrayal, the hurt she'd nursed through the past three years without him, she somehow didn't doubt his remorse.

She just wasn't sure remorse was enough to heal the rift between them.

"We were friends, Abby. No matter what else happened, that was real. Wasn't it?" The intensity of his gaze sucke punched her. For a second, the gulf between them seemed to narrow to nothing, and she felt herself drawn to him, magnet to steel.

She even took a couple of steps toward him, needing to feel his arms around her once again. It wasn't even sexual, not this time, just a burning need deep in her gut for the security and comfort she used to feel when Luke was around.

There had been a time when she'd felt as if Luke Cooper was her only real friend, the one person in the world who knew exactly who she was and what she needed.

But as he took a couple of answering steps toward her, she stopped herself short, dragging her gaze from his. "We were friends," she admitted grudgingly. "But so much has changed. I don't think we can depend on being friends like that again."

Luke stopped a few inches away from her. "I guess not."

She made herself smile. "At least we get the chance for a proper goodbye this time, huh?"

He stood there silently, not returning the smile.

She let hers fade, too. "We should get some sleep."

With a nod, Luke headed past her to the bedroom door. "Yeah. Early morning."

"How exactly are we getting out of here, anyway?" she asked, the safer subject giving her the courage to meet his gaze again. "You never said."

He smiled, his earlier tension seeping from his features. "You'll see in the morning."

She took a step closer to him, despite her earlier determination to keep her distance. The sudden light in his eyes sparked her curiosity. "Not even a hint?"

He walked back toward her, with each step seeming to fill more and more of the small bedroom until he was all she could see. He stood closer than before, close enough so that, had she reached out her hand, she could have laid it flat against the hard muscles of his chest. She clenched her fists at her side to keep them still.

He lowered his head toward her until his mouth was only an inch or two from her face. He took a slow, deep breath and whispered, "Not even a hint."

Then, brushing his lips lightly against her forehead, he turned around and left the room without another word.

Abby groped her way to the small single bed near the crib and sank heavily onto the mattress, her heart pounding. When she lifted her hand to her mouth, it was shaking.

How on earth would she be able to get through the next few days of 24/7 Luke Cooper?

## Chapter Six

Luke woke near daybreak and found the Pattersons up already, moving about the kitchen in near silence, apparently trying not to wake him. He sat up and stretched, surprised by how soundly he'd slept, and said good morning.

"Did we wake you?" Rita asked.

He assured her that they hadn't. "Please don't go to any trouble," he added, noticing that Rita was apparently about to cook breakfast. "We'll do fine with cereal or something—"

"She believes in a hearty breakfast. Once a Texan, always a Texan," Jim said, as if Rita's birthplace explained everything about her. Maybe it did. Abby was from Texas as well, her hardy practicality one of the things that had drawn him to her in the first place.

When his friend Matt had swept Abby off her feet and married her within weeks, Luke had understood. A girl like Abby wouldn't stay single long, and her sturdy sensibility made her an ideal Marine's wife.

He'd often wondered, especially these past three years, what would have happened had he met Abby first. Would he have been her husband instead of Matt?

The Marine Intel lifestyle made relationships difficult—constant travel from conflict zone to conflict zone, or base to base, wherever his investigative skills had been needed. And now, with Cordero's threat hanging over him like the sword of Damocles, he could never test the theory, even if they both wanted to.

"Have you told Abby how you're traveling yet?" Jim's eyes twinkled as he handed Luke a mug of strong, hot coffee.

"I thought I'd surprise her," Luke answered.

Jim winked and smiled. "I can think of worse companions to be cooped up with for the next few days."

Being cooped up with Abby and Stevie wouldn't be nearly as enjoyable as Jim thought. Maybe Jim sensed the familiarity between him and Abby, the result of several years of closeness before everything had gone to hell. Time hadn't erased the connection he felt to her. The second he'd discovered she needed him, there'd been no thought of saying no.

But when it was over, he'd walk away from her again to keep her safe. There was no other option. Not as long as Eladio Cordero was alive and in control of one of South America's biggest and most dangerous drug cartels.

"Go see if Abby's up," Rita called from the kitchen, where the smell of cooking biscuits was making Luke's stomach rumble with hunger. "She'll want these biscuits while they're hot."

Luke set the coffee mug on a coaster on the coffee table and headed down the hall to the nursery room. Pausing at the door, he listened for any sounds of stirring within. He caught the faint sound of happy babbling.

His lips curving with a smile, he eased the door open and softly called Abby's name. There was no answer.

He slipped inside. Abby was still asleep on the single bed, curled into a knot under the blanket. Stevie was awake, standing in his crib. He gave Luke a lopsided grin that made Luke's heart turn a flip.

He crossed to the crib. "Hey there, Little Bit."

Stevie held out his arms. "Down!" he demanded.

Luke picked him up and tucked him close, breathing in the

soft baby smell with a helpless grin. "Good grief, son, that diaper weighs a ton. What were you doing all night?"

Stevie reached up and patted Luke's jaw, a look of surprise on his face as his palm brushed against Luke's day's growth of beard. His mouth formed a small *O* and he rubbed his palm against Luke's cheek again.

"Tell you what, sport—what say we go to the bathroom and take care of your diaper and my beard?" He looked around the room for a diaper bag, but stopped short when his eyes locked with Abby's sleepy gaze.

"Has something happened?" Her voice was raspy with sleep.

"Just breakfast. Rita made biscuits. I think she might have been making gravy, too."

"She's from Texas originally," Abby said, sitting up. Her dark hair was a tousled but sexy mess.

Luke tried not to stare. "Did she tell you that?"

"Didn't have to. You know me and accents." She stretched her arms over her head, the motion tugging her T-shirt tight against her round, firm breasts.

"Down!" Stevie demanded loudly, his wriggling giving Luke a much needed distraction.

He set Stevie down on the floor, watching with a rush of affection as the child scooted across the bedroom to his mother's outstretched arms.

"Good grief, you need a diaper change, you little stinker!" Abby kicked the covers off and padded across the room in search of the diaper bag. The flannel pajama bottoms she wore fit snuggly against her curvy bottom, sending a little ache through him. He sucked in a quick breath.

Abby found the bag at the foot of the crib. "I'll be out for breakfast as soon as I clean him up and get the beds made."

"We're getting an early start, so pack up, as well." The little frown between Abby's eyes told him she'd caught the same raw gruffness in his words. "If you please," he added to soften the demand, and Abby's lips curved in a half smile.

He detoured to the bathroom down the hall to splash cold water on his face. He'd forgotten his razor, so shaving would have to wait until they were on the road.

He remembered the feel of Stevie's tiny hand on his face. He'd never considered having kids, despite coming from a large family, making a conscious choice years back to devote himself completely to his military service. He'd seen too many families destroyed by the pressures of the job he loved. He wasn't going to do that to a woman, much less to their children.

*But you're not in the corps anymore.*

*Maybe not,* he conceded to the treacherous voice in the back of his mind. But he'd never been in more danger than now.

ABBY FOLLOWED LUKE around the side of the Pattersons' house and stopped short, staring at the enormous tan-and-white Itasca Sunstar parked in the side driveway. The morning sun, peeking over the horizon to the east, tinted the recreational vehicle with a rosy glow, making the scene look like something out of an RV advertising brochure.

"Drives like a dream." Jim Patterson stood behind them, Stevie on his hip. "We just never have used it much. We keep talking about traveling the United States, but I guess we're just homebodies after all."

Stevie gazed with wonder at the RV. "Mama, look! Bus!"

Jim let him down and Stevie ran to Abby, lifting his arms up to be held. She picked him up and turned back to Luke, who stood by the open door of the RV.

He held out his hand. "Want to take a look inside?"

After a few seconds' hesitation, she put her hand in his

and let him help her up the step into the belly of the large, bus-shaped vehicle. His hand was warm and strong, achingly familiar despite the years of separation and estrangement. She forced herself to let go once she was safely inside, pressing her tingling fingers against Stevie's back.

She'd never been in this version of the Sunstar before and inspected it with curious interest, taking in the compact wall-to-wall furnishings, from the kitchen galley immediately to her left to the long sleeper sofa just opposite.

"Here's a shower—the bathroom—" Luke led her toward the back of the RV, through a narrow doorway into a cramped space almost completely filled by a queen-size bed. "I can sleep on the sofa up front. You and Stevie can sleep here."

It would be a semblance of privacy, thank goodness. It was going to be hard enough to keep her head around Luke on their cross-country journey without having to share motel rooms with him every night. They were lucky to have had the Pattersons to come to for help. She didn't know how she was ever going to be able to thank them for the risks they were taking.

"It's going to be okay," Luke murmured, his voice close enough to startle her. She turned and found him standing only a few inches away, his gaze warm and intense. He lifted his hand to her face, sliding a stray lock of hair out of her eyes.

"How can you know that?" she asked, closing her eyes against the power of his gaze. Her breath caught as his fingers slid down her cheek to settle in the curve of her neck.

"We've both been through worse. Haven't we?" Luke's voice lowered to a warm, liquid rumble.

An ache blossomed in the center of her chest, at both the sound of his voice, so centered and sure, and the silken seduction of his thumb gliding along the curve of her collarbone. "Yes." She knew he was thinking of all the times she'd suffered through the anxious wait for word from the battlefront.

But she was thinking about her pregnancy vigil, a maelstrom of hope, love, fear and loneliness. She'd never felt more alone, more unprepared for the challenges to come.

But she'd made it through the solitary wait, through the first years of single motherhood just fine. At least this time, she wasn't alone. Luke was there. It might not be the kind of relationship she'd imagined that one passionate night in his arms, but that dream had never been more than a sweet lie.

Somewhere behind them came the sound of a throat clearing. Abby backed away from Luke and turned to see Jim Patterson standing in the open doorway.

"Sorry to butt in, but we need to get this bus ready for travel. Rita's packing supplies to take with you so you won't have to stock up right away."

Abby looked at Jim's kind face and wanted to cry. "I don't know how to thank you."

"Just take care of yourselves," Jim answered. "And if you see my son and his family, give 'em a big hug and kiss for me."

"I will, I promise." The thought of reaching the other side of the country, where Luke's family would be waiting to help them any way they could, overwhelmed her to the point that she could barely hold back the flood of tears burning her eyes. Her voice choked with emotion. "I'll go help Rita."

She found Rita in the pantry, loading a large box with kitchen supplies. "There are pots, pans and dishes already stored in the RV," Rita told her as she placed a couple of spice bottles inside the box, "but no groceries."

"I can't believe the trouble you're going to for us." Abby set Stevie in one of the kitchen chairs. "Stevie, sit here just a second while Mama helps Miss Rita pack up for our adventure."

"Stevie, why don't you draw a picture for Mr. Jim and me to remember you by? Can you do that?" Rita retrieved a piece of paper and a blue highlighter pen from the phone desk. She put the pen and paper in front of Stevie and he went to work, his chubby hand wrapping around the highlighter with a death grip.

"He'll get that pen all over your table," Abby warned.

Rita shrugged. "It'll wash." She opened the flexible cooler sitting on a counter nearby and showed Abby the contents. "I packed some basics—frozen chicken fingers, several nice bluegill fillets from Jim's last fishing trip and some ground beef." Rita looked over at Stevie. "I also packed some macaroni and cheese—easy cheeseburger macaroni for Stevie. And a few canned goods—soup, vegetables and stuff a little boy will eat."

The tears Abby had fought all morning won the battle. She sank into the chair by Stevie, a soft sob escaping her throat.

Stevie looked up, a worried look on his face. "Mama?"

She buried her hot face in his neck. He patted her hair gently, clinging to her.

Rita handed her a tissue. "I'm a pretty good judge of character, Abby, so I can tell you this for sure. Luke Cooper is good people. He'll take care of you both."

Abby eased Stevie's arms from around her neck and re-settled him in her lap. "Believe me, that's the one thing about this whole mess I know already."

"I know you said he was your husband's best friend, but—" Rita's gaze shifted to look at Stevie.

"He was my friend, too," Abby said.

Rita gave her a considering look. "You have no idea what your husband could have been hiding?"

"My husband was always hiding something," she answered flatly. "It was his job. He never left that part of his work behind him when he came home."

"Luke worked the same sort of job, didn't he?"

She nodded. "He had to keep secrets, too. He just never seemed to relish it as much as Matt did."

"I think maybe you've learned how to keep a few secrets of your own," Rita murmured, her eyes on Stevie again.

Abby didn't answer the question written plainly on Rita's face. But a little knot formed in the center of her chest as she realized that Luke would start wondering the same thing about Stevie that Rita clearly was, sooner or later.

Probably sooner, given how much time they'd be spending in confined quarters on their trip across the country.

She had to tell him the truth, before he figured it out first. She didn't know if he'd forgive her for keeping such a secret, regardless of how he found out. But he deserved to hear it from her instead of someone else.

But she'd lived a lie so long, she didn't know how to tell Luke a truth she wasn't sure he'd want to hear.

THEY REACHED LA PALOMA RV Park near Las Cruces just before nightfall and not a moment too soon. Stevie, who'd been cheerful for most of the afternoon, was heading into cranky territory by the time Luke parked in an available slot with electric and water hookup. While Luke paid the fee and handled getting the Sunstar connected, Abby stayed behind to unpack a few of the essentials they'd need for their overnight stay.

As Luke approached the RV's side entrance, Stevie let out a loud, insistent wail. "No, mama! Want out!"

Luke couldn't blame the little guy. He'd been strapped in for most of the past nine hours. But he didn't need to be underfoot while his mother was working.

Abby's reply was gentle but firm. "Mama's got to set up for the night. Can you stay in your seat and watch Frogville for me? Just for a little while? Then I'll get you out."

"No Froggy! Out!"

Luke pulled himself into the RV and shot Abby a quick, questioning look. She was in the RV's galley, her hands full of plates. At his "may I?" gesture, she gave a little nod.

Luke bent and unstrapped Stevie from the car seat. "Come on, Stevie, let's go for a walk."

"Don't go far," Abby said. "I'll have the leftovers heated up in a few minutes." They'd bought extra food when they stopped in Tucson for lunch so they wouldn't have to worry about cooking dinner that evening. "Then I need to give Stevie his bath and put him to bed." She glanced toward the narrow shower compartment on the other side of the kitchen. "He's never had a shower before. Maybe it'll be fun for him."

The picture of Abby's sweet, curvy body slick with soap and water rose to Luke's mind at her words, and he dragged his gaze away from hers quickly, afraid she would see the hunger in his eyes. He tightened his grip on Stevie. "I'll bring him back in a flash," he said, his voice raspy and thick as he struggled against his body's treacherous response to the unbidden fantasy.

He hurried back outside the RV, lifting Stevie onto his shoulders. Stevie laughed excitedly, his tiny fingers gripping Luke's. "Ooo!" he said in a happy voice.

Luke tilted his head back to look up at Stevie. The boy grinned at him, his face washed gold by the setting sun, and what Luke saw in the little boy's face made his breath catch.

Stevie might have his mother's fair, freckle-dotted complexion and wide, expressive mouth, but he didn't have her smile. It wasn't Matt Chandler's smile, either.

That lopsided grin was all Cooper.

Son of a bitch. Stevie Chandler was his son.

Luke felt as if his legs were going to collapse beneath him. Spotting a picnic table a few yards away, he lowered Stevie to the ground and led him to the bench.

"Wanna ride!" Stevie insisted, trying to climb back on Luke's shoulders.

Luke halted the little boy's upward progress, cradling his small face between his own large, calloused hands. Now that he had seen himself in Abby's son, it was as if blinders had fallen away. Stevie's eyes were the same smoky gray as Luke's, flecked with the same mossy green. Stevie had Luke's thick, dark hair, straighter than Abby's headful of wavy ringlets, and the same set of dimples that he and all his brothers had been cursed with for the first twenty years of their lives, until age began to carve them into more masculine lines.

Stevie's expression began to grow troubled, and Luke quickly released him, soothing him with a soft pat to his back. "Did I scare you, sport?"

Stevie reached up and caught Luke's face between his soft, chubby hands, mimicking Luke's earlier action. He gazed up at Luke with serious concentration. Then he smiled, dimples back for an encore, and Luke couldn't breathe.

*My son,* he thought, the words branding his soul. He wanted to shout them aloud.

But he couldn't, he realized, his heart sinking. Not now.

Thanks to Cordero, maybe not ever.

ABBY HEATED THE leftover chicken nuggets from lunch in the RV's microwave, then appeased her maternal guilt by opening one of the cans of green peas that Rita had packed for them early that morning. By the time Luke returned with Stevie, she had dinner on the small dinette table across from the galley.

Stevie greeted her with a big, lopsided grin and held out his arms. "Mama!"

Abby took Stevie from Luke's arms and gave him a hug. "Look what's for dinner—chicken nuggets and green peas. Mmm."

"Mmm," Stevie echoed, patting her cheeks.

She looked up at Luke. "Was he good for you?"

Luke nodded, his expression pensive.

Something about Luke's subdued demeanor made her stomach give a little flip. "Is something wrong? Did something happen while you were out?" she asked.

Luke shook his head. "Everything's fine."

But she could see he wasn't telling the truth. Something had changed his whole mood in the short amount of time he and Stevie had been gone.

"Luke—"

"Let's eat, huh? Lunch was a long time ago." He patted his belly and grinned at Stevie, who beamed back at him.

"Eat!" he echoed.

Abby decided she'd misread Luke's mood, for he kept a grin on his face as he watched her settle Stevie in the booster seat Rita had lent them and set his plate in front of him. It had been a while since they'd been close enough to practically read each other's thoughts. Three years was a long time and a lot of experience. God knew, she'd changed, and she could tell that Luke was a different person now, as well.

Stevie grabbed the fork by his plate and stabbed at the chicken nuggets, making her smile. Her son, with his intelligent eyes and eager curiosity, was living proof of how much her own life had changed.

"He's just now learning to use utensils," she told Luke, taking the seat next to Stevie.

Luke sat opposite them, his gaze settled on Stevie. As Luke's grin faded to a look of intensity, Abby's earlier apprehension returned.

"Leftover chicken nuggets okay with you?" she asked nervously, overcome by the urge to break the uncomfortable silence.

Luke picked up his fork. "Just perfect." He started eating, one forkful after another.

Like a machine.

As Abby watched him finish off his portion of the left-overs, her own appetite fled, replaced by a knot of anxiety, lead-heavy, in the pit of her stomach.

Something was wrong.

# Chapter Seven

Night had fallen finally, dark and cool. Abby was putting Stevie to bed in the back, while Luke remained up front on the sofa, gazing idly at the television over the dashboard as he pondered what to do next.

Was he wrong about Stevie's paternity? He'd spent the past hour staring at the child, trying to see even a trace of Matt Chandler in his features, but all he'd seen were bits of Abby and himself.

Abby must know he was Stevie's father. Long before Matt's death, there'd been problems in their marriage, caused by Matt's lies—Matt himself had admitted his marriage was on the verge of collapse not long before his accident. Had Abby really slept with Matt shortly before his death, with the marriage about to crash and burn?

"Oh, my God."

He looked up sharply at the sound of Abby's voice. She stood near the galley, her arms wrapped around herself as if she were cold. Her hair, still damp from the shower, fell in curls around her scrubbed-clean face. She wore yoga pants and an oversize T-shirt that should have camouflaged her slender curves—but didn't. Luke felt his body grow taut and aware.

She wasn't looking at him, however. She was gazing at the television screen. He followed her gaze and saw a cable news reporter outside the same motel in Yuma that he and Abby had left the night before.

He grabbed the remote and thumbed off the mute button.

"—will not confirm reports that the unidentified male victim was this man, retired Marine Corps Major Luke Cooper, whose car was found at the scene." A headshot of Luke in uniform, from about four years earlier, flashed on the screen. "Attempts to contact Mr. Cooper have been unsuccessful."

"That's the room we were in." Abby's voice came out low and strangled. "Where the police tape is."

She was right. Yellow tape covered the door to the room he had rented the night before. But his Mustang was no longer parked in the lot in front of the room. "They must have impounded the Mustang for evidence." His calm voice sounded alien to his own ears. He didn't feel calm. He felt sick.

Because as the news camera zoomed in on the window of the motel room he and Abby had fled the night before, he spotted four curving slashes of rusty red painted across the grimy glass, forming the loose shape of a shark's head and dorsal fin.

He'd seen that mark before, in a dusty shanty town on the outskirts of Tesoro, Sanselmo's vibrant but dangerous capital city. There, working a tip from a disgruntled rebel, Luke and his small band of investigators had come across the scene of a brutal murder of a man, his wife and his three children. Painted on the walls and the windows in their blood, the same shark-shaped symbol had marked the work of the assassins.

*Los Tiburones.* The Sharks.

Eladio Cordero's enforcers.

"THINK THE MEN turned on each other? Maybe one killed the other?" Abby couldn't wrap her mind around the turn of events, and Luke's grim silence wasn't helping. "But why leave the body there?"

Luke stared at the now-muted television. The news broadcast had long since switched over to regular programming, some sort of sitcom, judging by the slapstick antics.

Abby paused in the middle of her restless pacing to look at him. "You're scaring me. Say something."

"I'm just trying to figure out what to do first."

"What do? What can we do?" Nervous energy sparked through her until she thought she would crawl out of her skin.

"The Yuma authorities will track down my family soon to see if they've heard from me. They'll be worried."

"Do you think the victim was one of the guys following us?"

"It's possible. But they were trained operatives."

"Maybe the killer was, too," she pointed out.

Luke's eyes narrowed slightly. "Maybe."

"Are two different groups after whatever Matt stole?" The remains of dinner sat like lead in her belly, making her queasy. It was bad enough to be in the crosshairs of one set of ruthless pursuers. If there was a different group out there trying to track them down—

"I don't think there's a connection," Luke said.

Abby stopped pacing. "Then it's a hell of a coincidence."

"They happen." Luke got up, grabbed his jacket from the back of the lounge chair and slipped it on.

"Where are you going?" she asked.

"I need some air."

She stared at him, more certain than ever that he was keeping something from her. He'd been acting funny since he came in for dinner. The news from Yuma had only made it worse.

"What aren't you telling me?" she asked.

He ran his hand over his jaw. The contact between his

palm and his beard stubble made a swishing sound, surprisingly loud in the silent belly of the RV. She felt his internal struggle like tangible energy swirling around them, sparking lightly through her nervous system. When he lifted his hand in wordless response and slipped out of the RV into the night, she felt as if something inside her had snapped.

Odd, she thought, to feel so connected to him again after all this time, after all that had torn them apart. Connected enough so that his clear rejection just now felt as if something had been ripped asunder inside her.

Almost from their first meeting, she'd felt drawn to Luke Cooper, first as Matt's Marine buddy, then as her own dear friend. Exactly when her feelings had changed from friendship to attraction, she wasn't sure. By the time it happened, she and Matt were already experiencing the trouble that would destroy their marriage, and she had long since begun hiding her emotions deep inside, as much to spare herself pain as to keep others from knowing her true feelings.

She'd certainly buried them too deep for self-analysis, so it had come as one hell of a shock that night hours after Matt's funeral, when a comforting embrace between two grieving friends had exploded into combustible desire.

After Luke had left her bed the next morning, never to return, she'd had plenty of time and distance to figure out the tangle of emotions Matt's death had unearthed. Like the fact that she'd been head over heels in love with her husband's best friend for far longer than she liked to admit.

She'd thought, for a few sweet hours, that he might feel the same for her.

But all that had happened since had proved her wrong.

"Hello?" Sam Cooper sounded wary over the phone. Luke wondered how much his brother already knew.

"It's me." He kept his voice low. Their campsite seemed to

be in the middle of the quickest route between more distant campsites and La Paloma's main building, where bathrooms, a public laundry and other amenities were located. Though most campers had already retired for the night, a few still wandered about in search of supplies and treats.

"Are you okay?" Sam asked. "We heard—"

"I know. I'm fine. We're fine."

"We?" Sam, alone among Luke's six siblings, knew the reason for Luke's self-imposed exile, how solitary Luke's life had become. His surprise was evident.

"Abby Chandler's with me."

"Where are you? No, don't tell me."

An ache had settled in the middle of Luke's chest, growing in intensity since his realization that he was Stevie's father. He'd hoped calling his brother would help him regain his focus. Sam had been his emotional safety valve since he'd forced the truth out of Luke a couple of years ago, after Luke had made the latest in a series of lame excuses to avoid going home. Sam had flown cross-country to confront Luke, who hadn't been able to keep the secret from his brother once they were face-to-face.

Sam had understood Luke's reasons for staying but insisted on keeping in touch. They used disposable phones, switching them out every time the minutes ran out. Luke had picked up his latest phone on a quick stop driving out of San Diego.

"I thought you wanted to stay as far from Abby as possible." Sam knew what had happened the night of Matt's funeral. Once Luke had confessed his biggest secret to his brother— Eladio Cordero's vow of vengeance—revealing his other secrets to Sam had been a relief.

"She has a son, Sam. Named Stevie." Luke swallowed hard. "He's two."

Sam's tone of voice changed immediately. "Yours?"

"Abby behaves as if he's Matt's."

"You haven't asked her directly?"

"We've been a little busy, what with the black-clad goons tossing our houses and *Los Tiburones* leaving their bloody calling cards on the window of the motel room we've just vacated." Luke looked around to make sure no one had overheard. "I'm not inclined to ask at the moment."

"Because of Cordero."

"I killed his son. If he knew I had a son of my own—"

"Got it," Sam said quickly. "Cordero's behind the murder in Yuma, right? I saw the mark on the window."

"I think so. But why now? Why Yuma? They haven't made a move toward me in almost three years. Not since Matt."

"You still believe the accident was murder?"

"Yes." Forensics hadn't been able to state, unequivocally, that the brakes had been tampered with. But Matt Chandler had been too good a driver to lose control of his car on a shallow incline the way he had, or hit the retaining wall at such a high speed that the car had folded like an accordion. "I'm just not as sure now that Cordero was behind it."

He condensed the events of the past couple of days for Sam, keeping an eye out for any campers paying too much attention to him as they wandered past the picnic table where he sat. "The goons in black throw a whole new wrinkle into Matt's death. But if they thought he had something on them, why wait three years to hunt down Abby? She wasn't in hiding. The only reason I can think of is that the investigation into Voices for Villages has made things a little too hot for someone."

"Any chance the men in black were *Los Tiburones*, too?"

"No, these guys definitely weren't Cordero's type of thugs. I'd guess ex-military."

"So, maybe connected to the gentleman from Foggy Bottom instead?" Sam asked.

"It's possible, isn't it? These guys might have been part of the arms-for-drugs market I was investigating." Luke's head was beginning to throb with weariness and stress. He'd been anticipating Cordero's next move against him for a long time. That it had coincided with the threat to Abby and Stevie was a nightmare. "Weird that Sanselmo figures into both of my problems, isn't it?"

"Has me wondering if it's just a coincidence. The arms network sold to *El Cambio.* Cordero's cartel helps finance *El Cambio,*" Sam pointed out.

"But we never found any direct connection between the gunrunners and Cordero himself. Believe me, I looked for it." Luke leaned forward on the picnic table bench, tucking his coat closer around him. The temperature was dropping rapidly now that the sun had set. He needed to get back into the RV soon, before Abby started to worry.

"Well, I've got a new wrinkle for you, one that may explain why it took this long for someone to start looking for whatever it is that Matt Chandler stole. Janis Meeks has dropped off the radar. She's cleared out her office, and nobody at Voices for Villages is saying why, or where she might be."

Luke clutched the phone more tightly. "And now there are people looking for some mysterious thing Matt may have stolen."

"I can't think that's a coincidence," Sam added.

"No," Luke agreed. "But the question is—did she drop off the radar on her own, or was she pushed?"

"Maybe you should stop worrying about who's connected to whom and just concentrate on keeping clear of everybody who's after you," Sam said firmly. "Do you have a plan?"

"Yeah. I think in cases like these, there's safety in numbers." Luke smiled at the image that rose in his mind of himself, his brothers and his feisty sister, running around the lake house driving his parents insane. Like all siblings, they'd bickered and fought, but let anyone outside the family give any one of them trouble, and they were all on the same team.

"Does that mean what I think it means?"

"Yeah," Luke said, his smile fading quickly. Even though he knew it was his only choice, the last thing he wanted was to make his family a target of Cordero's brutal sense of justice. And just being around him was putting Abby and Stevie in double danger. "But I wish there was another choice. I wish—" He stopped, rubbing his hand over his tired eyes. "I wish I could put Abby and Stevie on the next bus to God knows where and get as far away from them as I can. I don't need this headache on top of everything else. God knows, they don't need me."

"I think you're wrong about that," Sam answered. "I've been telling you all along that you don't need to make yourself an exile just because Cordero's gunning for you."

Luke wanted to believe Sam was right. But if anything happened to the people he loved—

"Listen, I've got to run. Kristen and Maddy are waiting for me to start the DVD. It's princess night again."

Luke could hear Sam's eyes rolling, but he also couldn't miss the overpowering love in his brother's voice when he spoke of his daughter and his new wife.

"Okay," he said, just about to ring off when a new, horrifying thought occurred to him. "Wait, Sam—call Hannah. Her in-laws need to take a trip ASAP to somewhere where they're surrounded by people they can trust." If *Los Tiburones* could find the motel in Yuma, there was a chance they could have tracked Luke to his next destination. He couldn't bear it if something happened to the Pattersons because they'd gone out of their way to help him ånd Abby.

"Already done," Sam answered quickly. "They saw the newscast, made the connection and felt the sudden urge to roam. They should have been on the road a couple of hours ago."

"Thank God." Luke breathed a long sigh of relief. "If you hear from them again, thank them. And apologize for me."

"Take care of yourself, Luke."

"Thanks, Sam." He rang off before the hot burning behind his eyes turned into something more embarrassing. Tucking the phone in his pocket, he headed back inside the RV.

Abby was sitting cross-legged on the sofa bed, her tense gaze lifting to meet his the second he walked through the door. "What the hell's going on, Luke?"

"Nothing," he lied, then softened the deceit with a bit of truth. "I called my brother Sam to let him know I was okay."

"I thought we weren't supposed to use our cell phones."

He pulled the disposable phone from his pocket and waved it at her. "Disposable. Picked it up back in San Diego when I bought some supplies for the trip. Nobody knows to trace it."

"Oh. Is everybody back home okay?"

He felt guilty because he hadn't asked that question directly. But Sam would have told him if anyone in the family was in some kind of trouble. "Yeah. Seem to be."

She unlocked her fingers, which had been clasped tightly in her lap, flexing her joints as if they'd grown stiff. "I've been sitting here imagining the worst."

He sat beside her on the sofa. She scooted over to make room but stayed close enough so that he could feel her body heat, warm and inviting, against his side. "Because I didn't tell you where I was going?"

Her smile was a little self-conscious. "I guess I should be used to being out of the information loop by now."

He turned to look at her. "No, I should have told you." He probably would have stopped long enough to tell her his plan had he not been so blindsided by the realization that Stevie was almost certainly his son.

He wanted to ask her for the truth. The question burned on his tongue. But he'd meant what he'd told Sam—he didn't want to know for sure. Not right now. It was better for all of them to table the question as long as Cordero was gunning for him.

"Luke, there's something I need to tell you about Stevie—"

*No,* he thought, *don't say it.* "He's okay, right?" Luke stood up, putting distance between them. He headed toward the back of the RV, where Abby had earlier set up a place on the bed for Stevie to sleep, since they'd had to leave the crib behind in Yuma. He found the small boy curled up between two pillows, sleeping peacefully.

His heart clutched, the breath leaking from his lungs. His son. In the low light from the RV cabin, Stevie's sleeping face seemed almost as familiar as the face Luke saw every morning in the mirror. How had it taken him so long to see the resemblance?

*You didn't want to,* a quiet voice in his mind reminded him. *Claiming him as your son is too dangerous.*

"He's fine," Abby said quietly behind him.

He turned to look at her. Her dark curls were still damp from the shower, and her face was scrubbed shiny clean. She'd donned a pair of loose-fitting sweatpants and an old Padres T-shirt that had seen its best days a long time ago, but he'd never seen anything more beautiful in his life.

God, he'd missed her. Her quirky sense of humor, her quick mind, her feisty spirit—all of the things that had drawn him to her the minute Matt introduced them. She'd been off-limits as anything but a friend while Matt was alive, of course, but he'd found himself willing to take those crumbs from her as long as he didn't have to say goodbye.

He'd been through hell and back a dozen times over, in any number of dangerous global hot spots, but walking away from Abby's bed had been the hardest thing he'd ever done.

And sooner or later, God help him, he was going to have to walk away from her again.

Maybe he should go ahead and do what he told Sam—drop her and Stevie off at the nearest bus stop, hand them all the cash he had on hand and tell them to run as far from civilization as they could get.

But as strong and smart as Abby was, she was no match for the men who had broken into his house the day before. And while he got the feeling those men weren't going to indulge in violence for its own sake, he didn't doubt they were ruthless enough to grab Stevie and use him to torment Abby.

He couldn't let that happen. Not to Abby.

Not to his son.

Abby's eyes narrowed as she looked up into his face, as if she was reading the storm of thoughts swirling behind his eyes. He tried to clear his expression, but she was always more perceptive than was good for her.

"Do you think I don't know there's something else going on with you?" Her voice was soft and low, but there was steel running through it.

He cupped her elbow and led her away from the bedroom area. She pulled away when they reached the front, turning to face him with fire in her eyes.

"I spent eight years living with a man whose every word was a cipher. I could never be sure of the truth, even when he spoke it. So please, Luke, don't lie to me. I don't care how hard the truth is, I want to hear it."

*Tell her,* another voice whispered in his mind, a completely different voice from the hard voice that had warned him of the dangers of letting Stevie into his life. This was the voice that had talked to him the night of Matt Chandler's funeral, the one that told him the light shining in Abby's eyes when she gazed up at him in that darkened living room was more than just friendship.

Abby's expression shifted suddenly, and he knew she'd read him again. She knew he was keeping things from her and felt the implicit rejection of his deceit, even if she didn't understand the true reason for it.

She turned suddenly to leave, and even though his brain was screaming at him to let her go, he couldn't keep from reaching out to hold her in place. He closed his hands around her arms, pulling her back around to face him.

At her soft gasp, he eased his grip, but he didn't let her go. He slid one hand up her arm and over the curve of her shoulder, brushing his fingertips over the ridge of her collarbone. Thrilling at the softness of her heated skin, he lifted his forefinger and placed it against her throat to feel the wild hammering of her pulse.

"Luke." He could tell by her look of consternation that she'd intended the word to convey protest, not the sweet seduction that spilled from her lips instead. She tried to pull away from him, but even though he knew he should let her go, his grip tightened on her arm again.

She gave in. He saw it in the softening set of her mouth, the liquid surrender in her eyes. He felt color bloom over her throat, hot beneath his touch. When he bent closer, she moved in response, until her breasts brushed against his ribcage, setting his body ablaze.

Nothing on earth could have stopped him from kissing Abby Chandler in that moment.

Nothing but the loud trill of the disposable cell phone.

With a groan, he stepped back and grabbed the phone, his gaze locked with Abby's. Her eyes were heavy-lidded and dark, her respiration rapid. She licked her lips and looked away.

"Yeah?" he answered the phone, not caring that his voice was gruff.

It was Sam, of course. He sounded grim. "You need to get back on the road, Luke. As soon as possible."

Luke tightened his grip on the phone. "Why? What's happened?"

"Someone firebombed the Pattersons' house three hours ago."

## Chapter Eight

Luke's horrified expression felt like a punch to Abby's gut. He paced away from her, his movements quick and angry. "How did that happen, Sam? Are they okay?"

Abby wished she could hear the other end of the conversation. Luke's reaction was scaring the hell out of her.

"Thank God. Are they under police protection?"

Had someone gotten to Luke's family? She moved closer to him, braving the anger radiating from him like heat waves. "What is it?" she whispered.

He rested his hand on the side of her neck. "The Pattersons' house was firebombed," he murmured. "They're okay."

The remains of Abby's dinner rose in the back of her throat. Swallowing hard, she dropped to the sofa and gazed up at Luke, flames of guilt licking at her gut.

It was her fault. She'd brought this nightmare into their lives. Into Luke's. She should have handled things on her own. For God's sake, she'd been married to Matt for eight years. She should have fought harder to make him share more of his life with her. Then, maybe, she'd have half a clue what the hell these people were after.

"No, that's a good idea. I don't think there's anywhere to hide from these people for long. Better to go somewhere that they'll have backup." Luke's hand remained, warm and strong, against her neck, his thumb sliding absently over her collarbone in a rhythmic caress that stoked the simmering flame he'd started a few minutes earlier. She pulled away from him, horrified that she could feel aroused in the middle of this newest crisis. What was wrong with her?

"I agree. We stay on the move as much as possible." Luke gave her another quick look. "Thanks for the call. I'll check back as soon as we're on the road." He rang off. "I'm sorry. We've got to start prepping the RV for travel again."

"Are you sure the Pattersons are okay?"

He nodded. "They were out in the garage when it happened, getting the car ready to head out of town. Someone drove by and threw Molotov cocktails through their front windows. They were able to get out of the garage and to safety."

"Did they save the car?"

"Yeah. The fire didn't spread much behind the front two rooms. As soon as they gave their statement to the police, and secured the house as well as they could, they headed north. They're going to visit old friends in Wyoming."

"Thank God." Abby grabbed Luke's arm as he took a couple of steps toward the galley. "You didn't get nearly as much sleep last night as I did. I'll drive."

"Driving an RV isn't like driving a car—"

"My dad used to sell RVs back in Texarkana. I learned to drive rigs bigger than this one by the time I was sixteen." She released his arm. "Haven't I ever told you that before?"

"You never talked much about your family," he said quietly.

She supposed she hadn't. Losing both of her parents in a plane crash shortly after high-school graduation had been devastating. She rarely spoke of it, or the eighteen short years she'd had with them.

She'd have to get over that now. Her parents were Stevie's grandparents, even if they weren't around anymore. They might be the only grandparents he ever heard about. He would need some sense of his heritage.

*But doesn't he also deserve to know his father? His aunts and uncles? His grandparents on Luke's side?*

She ignored the question. "So I'll drive," she said again. "You kick back, try to get some sleep."

He shrugged, which she took as assent. "Let's get to work," he said.

Within an hour, they'd locked down anything in the RV likely to move around during travel. Stevie was already asleep again after stirring briefly while Abby had buckled him into his car seat, and Luke had finished unhooking the RV from the park's hookups and returned to the RV cabin.

He settled into the passenger seat, laid his head back against the headrest and closed his eyes.

"Just head north to Albuquerque on I-25?" she asked.

He nodded. "Then east on I-40 when you get there. And keep to the speed limit. We don't need to be pulled over."

"It'll be a strain," she murmured, buckling herself in. "You know my lead foot."

He opened one eye, his lips curving. "Yeah. I was on that trip to Monterey, remember?"

"I remember." The trip to Monterey had been early in her marriage, when she still believed she and Matt had a chance at making their relationship work, but the strongest memory of the day was how Luke had taken her to the Defense Language Institute to introduce her to one of his former instructors. Matt had deemed the proposed side trip boring and headed to Del Monte Beach without them. Matt had never been the type to put aside his own passions to accommodate someone else's.

It had fallen to Luke to take her to the Defense Language Institute and wait patiently while she talked shop with his old language instructor, even though he wasn't much more interested in the topic than Matt had been. She was pretty sure she'd started nursing a secret crush on Luke that sunny day in Monterey when Luke had forgone a trip to a beach full of bikini-clad beauties just for her.

"I always figured you'd end up working there." Luke's voice sounded a little drowsy, as well. "Why didn't you?"

"How do you know I didn't?" she asked.

He glanced toward her. It was dark in the cabin, but she thought he looked a little guilty. "I guess I don't," he murmured, a little too nonchalantly, closing his eyes again.

She turned her gaze back to the road, surprised by what he'd unwittingly revealed. The only way he'd know that she'd never fulfilled her dream of working at the institute was if he'd looked for her there. Had he checked up on her sometime in the past three years? It wouldn't have been that hard to find her—he could have called any of the women she'd befriended during her time as a Marine wife.

Unless he hadn't wanted her to know he was checking on her.

She didn't know what would be worse—his simply putting her out of his mind altogether after their one brief night together, or his making the effort to find out about her while doing his damnedest to hide his interest. Either way, he still kept his distance for three years. Did it really matter why?

She turned her focus back to the road ahead. Luke hadn't given her any instructions, other than heading east. But she knew that the people who'd been following them had been able to stay on their trail pretty closely so far. If they had already figured out where she and Luke were headed, they might have people staking out the interstates, waiting for them to drive right into the trap.

She wasn't about to let that happen.

Reaching the cloverleaf on North Main Street that led to the I-25 on-ramp, she made a snap decision to keep going on Highway 70 running east, bypassing the interstate altogether.

Even sticking to the speed limit, she could have them in Texas by morning.

"DID REID KNOW about the price on Cooper's head before he sent us on this mission?" Tris snapped open the Colt M119 cleaning kit and started to work, anger evident in his every movement. As usual, his upper-crust Boston accent slipped a little when he was upset, revealing his Southie roots. Tris had changed everything about himself—his name, his accent, his manners—when he'd been recruited into one of the government's most secret of secret agencies several years ago. But some things a man could never change completely.

Damon knew. He'd made a few changes of his own—new name, fancy education, better wardrobe—but nothing could change the fact that he'd been born Demetrius Miles in a run-down housing project in Birmingham, Alabama. His mother had never married the succession of men who kept her in bruises and babies, and though she'd made sure Damon got to school and did his homework every day, she herself lacked the education to give him a leg up on his academic studies.

But Damon had been blessed with a quick mind and a strong body. He'd gone to school on the G.I. bill, working hard to overcome the deficits of his previous schooling. His stint in the Marines had taken him to Virginia and the man who'd become his mentor.

The man who'd assigned him to his current mission.

"It's hard to imagine he didn't," Damon answered aloud. He knew the government kept tabs on Cordero's cartel. They'd know whether or not Cordero had a reason to want Luke Cooper dead. And if the government knew, Barton Reid knew. Knowledge was currency to him. He knew things even the government didn't.

"Grady was a good man," Tris growled. "We should've been warned of the possibility of ambush."

Damon didn't know if forewarning would have been enough. Grady and Samuelson had been trained to handle anything that might arise during a snatch-and-grab mission. But all the training in the world could be trumped by a force of men with little regard for the rules of engagement and the advantage of surprise, as any number of guerrilla wars had proved over the years.

Grady had gone down immediately, and Samuelson had been forced to fight his way out, sustaining life-threatening injuries. Luckily, he'd had a chance to call in an extraction team before his comm gear had been smashed. Damon, Tris and others in the crew had found him holed up in an abandoned building a couple of blocks from the motel, weak from blood loss. *Los Tiburones* were long gone by then, having had their fun with Grady after they discovered their real prey had already flown the coop.

"Not the only thing Reid has neglected to tell us," Tris added blackly. "Must be a hell of a secret he's keeping."

It would make their assignment much easier to know what Chandler had taken from Reid. But Reid hadn't kept his position in life by sharing his secrets. Quite the opposite, Damon suspected. He was sure Reid had risen so quickly in the Foreign Service ranks by using other people's secrets against them.

"Any word from the guys in the field?" he asked aloud.

Tris shook his head. "We have units positioned along the interstate highways out of Yuma, but nobody's spotted them yet."

As of their last mission briefing three hours earlier, nobody had yet figured out how Cooper had escaped the motel with a civilian woman and baby and disappeared into the night. His biographical dossier showed no close contacts in the Yuma,

Arizona, area. Apparently the powers that be were so worried about losing track of Cooper and Abby Chandler that when Damon joked that they'd called a cab, someone had been assigned to contact all the cab companies in town.

Whatever Reid was looking for, it must be big. Bring down the administration big, maybe. That kind of information was like gold in political circles.

Or poison.

Either way, Damon intended to be the one to find it.

MOONLIGHT SLANTED *in from the window, bathing Abby's body in a soft blue glow that made her pale skin gleam like polished alabaster. Luke's heart contracted as he stood by the bed, poised between surrender and flight.*

Stay or go? *It was always the question, wasn't it?*

*His body still hummed from the aftermath of their passion, and in her soft, delicate curves he read the promise of endless nights spent wrapped in each other. Both lovers and friends, sharing fire and sweetness. Men spent their whole lives looking for exactly what lay before him.*

*But in his gut, he knew the costs would be too high.*

*He waited for her to stir, needing to talk to her one more time before he walked out of her life for good. But she lay motionless, as still and pale as a Grecian sculpture bathed in moonlight. He found himself bending to touch her to see if she'd turned to stone in the night, but he paused with his hand inches from her arm.*

*His skin prickled, as if a cold finger had traced a warning on his spine.* "Abby?" *he whispered.*

*She didn't move.*

*His hand trembled as he reached out to touch her shoulder. She felt cold to his touch. Too cold.*

*He knelt on the bed and cupped her face where it lay on the pillow. Something sticky clung to his fingers.*

*His heart stuttering in his chest, he turned her face toward him and saw her sightless stare. Something black and wet stained the pillow where she lay.*

*Only then did he see the dark, jagged ribbon of blood across her throat.*

*"Abby!" He grabbed her, shook her hard. She gave no resistance, limp in his grip. His heart fluttered against his chest, ravaged by grief and the acid of guilt. He laid her back on the pillow, lifting shaking hands to close her eyes.*

*"I'm sorry," he moaned, taking one of her cold hands in his. "I'm so sorry."*

*Her eyes snapped open, and her lips parted. Air passed through her mouth in a dying hiss. "Too late."*

Luke jerked awake, his heart galloping. It took a second to reorient himself, to escape the cottony prison created from the potent elixir of bittersweet memories and fear. As the vivid images of his dream faded, he realized he was in the Pattersons' RV, belted into the passenger seat. Abby sat in the driver's seat next to him, her eyes slanting his way for a moment at his stirring.

"You okay?"

He stared at her for a moment, too overcome with relief to answer immediately. He drank in the reality of the pink stain of health in her cheeks, evident even in the pale lights from the RV dashboard. He just watched her breathe for a moment, in and out in steady cadence. Even the way she was looking at him, as if he'd lost his mind, was a welcome sight.

"I'm fine," he managed. "Just a bad dream, I guess."

"What was it about?"

"Can't remember," he lied, pushing himself up from his slumped position. "Are we on I-40 already?"

"I didn't go north to Albuquerque," she answered. "I got to thinking about it—the people after us probably have connections all over the country. They may have people staking out the interstates. So I took a less obvious route east."

The dashboard clock read 4:24 a.m. "Where are we?"

"Just crossed the state line into Texas near Plains."

"Good thinking." He should've thought of taking an alternate route himself. He needed to get his head together and focus on a plan. He just didn't have much experience running away from danger. He was the guy who was usually leading the pack straight into the mouth of hell.

He twisted around to look at Stevie. The little fellow was sleeping soundly, seemingly unbothered by being strapped into the car seat like a papoose.

Luke envied his innocence. Stevie was still young enough to see this whole thing as an adventure. He'd been good for them on the drive from Yuma to Las Cruces, singing songs with Abby and proving himself to be a lot better-natured than Luke would have been at his age, if his mother's stories were anything to go by.

*Definitely got your mama's good nature instead of your daddy's, huh, Little Bit?*

"Is he always so easygoing?" he asked Abby, the need to know more about Stevie overcoming his intention to keep his emotional distance. "He's been such a good trooper."

"He's usually happy. He likes to laugh." Abby's voice swelled with affection. "Life isn't always stable with us—working freelance as much as I do, my schedule can be irregular. And without steady job benefits like a pension or insurance, I've had to pay for a policy for us out of my own pocket."

"How did you do it?"

"I still had some money from the sale of my parents' RV dealership—I'd kept that rolling over in investments for a while, but after Matt died and I had a baby on the way, I had to start drawing on it to supplement my income. There's a little

left. Not a lot. I was already planning to look for a full-time
job when all of this happened."

He looked over at her. She looked tired, wrung-out and
sleep-deprived, but he still found himself wanting to drag her
from behind the wheel and pull her into his arms to finish
what they'd almost started the night before.

The phantom image of death and despair from his earlier
nightmare flashed through his head, saving him from saying
something he'd shouldn't. He turned his gaze back to the flat,
barren highway illuminated in the RV's headlights.

West Texas sprawled around him, punctuated by scrubby
stands of winter-bare trees and the occasional farmhouse or
outbuilding. Power poles lined the highway like silent soldiers
standing guard. "How much farther to Lubbock?"

"A couple of hours. We can stop there for breakfast."

Luke didn't want to think about food. He was still queasy
from the aftereffects of his dream about Abby. But they had
a lot of miles stacked up ahead of them, and food was fuel,
as he'd learned in the Marines Corps.

His feelings were irrelevant. Marines did their duty. His
duty was to get Abby and Stevie to safety and help them find
out what Matt had been hiding.

And that's what he'd do, come whatever hell that may.


LUKE AND ABBY traded driving duties over the course of
the long day, managing naps here and there to keep up their
stamina. Stevie, on the other hand, was quickly beginning to
tire of life on the road. Right now, he was occupied watching
cartoons on the RV's television set, but Abby didn't know how
much longer they could keep traveling without stopping for
more than a few minutes at a time every few hours.

She was also beginning to second-guess the decision to
borrow the Pattersons' RV, now that they were wary of stopping at any more RV parks. It was next to impossible to blend

into traffic driving the massive vehicle. Their pursuers had probably connected the firebombing in Yuma to their escape already. How long before they had the license plate number for the RV and put out a phony all points bulletin?

"We need to switch license plates," Abby said a little while later, after bringing up her concerns to Luke. "Except there's no way I'm going to risk someone else's life that way."

"Ideally, we'd switch tags with the same make and model of RV, one that's similar in color and not currently in use." Luke slanted a lopsided grin at her. "Of course, ideally, I'd have a billion dollars and a red Ferrari."

The sight of his grin made her heart turn an embarrassing little flip. She dragged her gaze back to the road. "Can't help you with either of those. If my folks were still alive, though—" She stopped short as an idea popped into her head.

"What?" Luke prodded.

She grinned at him, feeling hopeful for the first time in days. "I know where we can find that license plate we need."

## Chapter Nine

The sign over the sales lot read Seymour Motor Homes of Tex-arkana. Sunset had passed, only a faint smear of blood orange on the horizon as a reminder of their long day. Luke looked over at Abby, who gazed at the sign with a hint of sadness in her tired blue eyes. "This was your folks' place?"

She nodded. "Billy didn't even change the name."

"How long since you've seen the place?"

She turned into the lot and parked. "Ten years. I left when my parents died and haven't been back since."

"Are you sure Billy's still here?"

"I got a letter on my birthday. He mentioned he was taking good care of the place." Abby sounded different when she spoke of Billy Langston, the man she'd sold her parents' RV dealership to after their death. As she'd neared her hometown, her East Texas accent, softened by time and distance, had found its edge again. "Go see if he's still here. There might be people around who'd remember me."

"Will he come back with me? Won't he think it's a trick?"

She smiled brightly. "Tell him Baby Abigail sent you."

He grinned. Baby Abigail?

He stepped down from the motor home and out into the mild November night, glad to stretch his legs and breathe in something besides diesel fumes and the fragrant remains of their fast-food meals. Glancing back at the RV, he saw Abby had left the driver's seat and disappeared from view.

He approached the dealership office in long strides, pasting a friendly smile on his tired face when a stocky man in his late fifties stepped out of the office to greet him before Luke reached the door.

"We're closed for the evenin'," the man said firmly in a wide Texas drawl.

"I'm looking for Billy Langston. Is he still here?"

The man's expression grew wary. "I'm him."

"Baby Abigail sent me. She's waiting in the RV over there." Luke motioned toward the Pattersons' RV.

Langston's dark eyes slanted toward the vehicle, his expression instantly suspicious. "Who the hell are you?"

"Her friend."

Langston looked him over. "Do you have a name, friend?"

Luke glanced back at the RV, feeling exposed. "Did someone come here and tell you something about Abby?"

"Tell Baby Abigail to come out here where I can see her."

The back of Luke's neck prickled. "Is someone else here?"

"You think I'd tell you?"

Luke sighed. "I don't know what you've been told—"

Billy brushed past him and walked toward the RV. "Abigail? You in there?"

"Mr. Langston—" Luke caught up with him. "We're trying to keep a low profile, sir."

Langston wheeled on him. "That's what I hear."

"What exactly do you hear?"

Langston frowned. "Abigail's inside there? For true?"

"Yes."

His gaze narrowed on Luke. "Why didn't she come herself?"

"She didn't know if you'd be here alone. There's a reason she doesn't want people to know where she is."

"Because of the murder in Yuma?" Langston squared his shoulders. "What've you gotten the girl into, mister?"

"He's helping me, Billy."

Luke and Billy Langston both turned at the sound of Abby's soft voice. She stood beside the RV, Stevie propped on one hip, gazing at Langston with a mixture of love, sadness and relief in her blue eyes.

"Hey, Billy," she said, her lips curving into a grin.

"Baby Abigail." Langston took a step toward her, his heart in his eyes. "Good Lord, girl, you grew up on me."

She handed Stevie to Luke and held out her arms to Langston. "What's it take around here for a girl to get a hug?"

Stevie squirmed in Luke's arms, twisting around to look at his mother hugging a stranger. He started to cry. "Mama!"

"Shh, son, it's okay. Mama's just fine," Luke crooned.

Langston released Abby. "Is this your boy?"

"That's Stevie." Abby smiled at her son. "He's a pistol."

"You had a baby and never told us?"

Abby's face fell. "It was complicated. Matt had died only a little time before—"

Billy smiled. "He looks like you."

Luke stroked Stevie's back soothingly. "I hate to break up the reunion, but we're pretty exposed—"

"Let's get y'all into the office. There's nobody else here. It'll be safe." Langston nodded his head for them to follow him back to the sales office. Luke tucked Stevie close and took up the rear, keeping an eye out in case Abby was wrong about trusting her father's old friend. Someone had been here already, looking for them. It could be a trap.

But the sales office was empty, just as Langston said. He

led them to a small room in the back and waved at the comfortable-looking sofa across from a battered oak desk. "Sit down. Y'all look like hell."

"It's been a stressful couple of days," Abby admitted.

"Someone's been here asking about us," Luke told her. "Mr. Langston thinks I've done something to get you in trouble."

"It's not Luke," Abby said quickly to Langston. "I'm the one who dragged Luke into this."

She explained quickly about arriving home to her apartment to find it occupied by masked men looking for something her late husband had apparently taken.

"And you've got no idea what it was?" Langston asked.

"None."

"Who came to see you?" Luke asked.

Langston shot a look at him. "Said they were FBI. Can't say I'm quite as sure now they were telling the truth as I was when they flashed their badges at me."

"What did they say?"

"Seems like you're a suspect in a murder back in Arizona." The look Langston shot him suggested he wasn't entirely sure the accusation wasn't true.

"Luke didn't kill anyone," Abby said. "Those men were after us, not the other way around."

Luke's phone rang, making Abby jump beside him. He handed Stevie over to her and dug in his pocket for the disposable phone. He didn't recognize the number on the display.

"Yeah?" he answered carefully.

"Luke, it's me." It was Sam. Luke relaxed. "I bought a new phone. I think you might want to do that as well, next chance you get."

"Has something new happened?"

"Just an APB out of Yuma, Arizona, looking for you in connection to a murder at a motel there."

"Yeah, we heard about that already."

Sam's wry tone changed immediately. "How? Did someone try to pick you up?"

"Not yet. We ran into an old friend of Abby's. Someone claiming to be FBI paid him a visit. I'm not sure it was really the Feds, though."

"Your friends in black?"

"Or someone like them."

"Right now, you're just a person of interest because you left your car at the motel right in front of the room where the murder took place. Kristen had her partner, Jason, ask for more information on the murder. She's going to see how much they're really working with so we'll know better what to do next."

Luke's heart sank as the reality of his dilemma sunk in. "I can't come home. They'll be looking for me there."

"You can't stay out there on the road, either, Luke. But I think you need to ditch the RV as soon as you can. Someone finally got around to connecting you to the Pattersons, thanks to the firebombing of their home. The APB lists the Pattersons' RV as a possible vehicle of interest."

Luke's stomach dropped. No matter how many times they zigzagged, the bad guys stayed right behind them. Or, hell, maybe in front of them by now. No telling at this point. He hid his growing despair. "Okay, we'll figure out something."

"Just get to Alabama. Call me when you cross the state line and we'll go from there." Sam rang off.

"What is it?" Abby's eyes gleamed with anxiety.

"We've got to ditch the RV. It's included on the APB."

Abby's lower lip started to tremble. She caught it between her teeth and lifted her chin, her eyes darting around as if she could somehow find the answer to their latest disaster of a problem somewhere in the RV sales office.

Her gaze settled on Billy Langston. "Did you sell your car dealership or give it to Ross?"

Langston seemed taken aback by the laser focus of her gaze. "I still own it. I split my time between the dealerships."

Abby's expression cleared, and she actually broke into a big smile of relief. "Great! Can we borrow an SUV?"

ABBY HADN'T REALIZED just how much she'd missed Texas until she walked into the Langstons' kitchen and saw Wanda Langston standing in front of their ancient gas stove, stirring a big pot of turnip greens and whistling an old Dolly Parton tune. She turned at the sound of Billy's boots clomping on the floor as he stepped inside behind Abby, Stevie and Luke. Her eyes widened and her weathered face split with an enormous grin.

"Abigail!" She crossed to Abby, her arms outstretched.

Abby flung herself into the woman's arms, overwhelmed by the familiar scent of White Linen and cooking greens.

Except for a few more gray hairs sprinkled through her close-cropped auburn curls and a few more smile lines, Wanda hadn't changed a bit in the past ten years. She was short and compact, muscular from working in her garden and tending to the chickens and pigs she raised for extra income. Her hands were rough in texture but gentle as a mother's touch as she cradled Abby's face to get a better look. "Good God, girl, you're too thin. Don't they feed you out in California?"

Abby blinked back tears and grinned. "Not as well as you do!" She gave Wanda another hug. "It's so good to see you."

Wanda looked at Billy. "Couldn't call ahead, old man?"

Billy grinned back at her. "I wanted to surprise you."

Wanda made a face at her husband, then looked at Luke, who stood to the side, holding Stevie on one hip. Wanda's smile faded a little. "You must be the fellow who's put our Abigail crossways with the law."

Luke's eyebrows notched upward. "Looks that way."

Wanda gave him a long, considering look. "Well, you'd better be worth the headache."

"I'm the one who put *him* crossways with the law, Wanda." Abby caught Wanda's hands. "Luke was in the Marines with Matt."

Wanda's eyes narrowed at her mention of Matt's name. Most people had liked Matt as soon as they met him. He'd been that kind of guy, charming, funny and impossible to resist in a lot of ways. But Wanda had never warmed to him the handful of times she had visited Abby in California. Abby had always figured it was because Wanda blamed Matt for keeping Abby out West after her college days were done. She knew Wanda had thought Abby would head back home to Texas after school. When it didn't happen, Matt had been as good a scapegoat as any.

Although, knowing Wanda's keen insight into people, maybe she'd seen what even Abby hadn't seen until much later—the liar and cheater hidden beneath Matt's pleasing exterior.

Abby crossed and took Stevie from Luke's arms. Luke gave her an odd look, as if he were seeing her for the first time. Maybe he was, in a way. When her parents died, she'd let the move to California for school create an almost complete break from her old life. It had been the only way she could survive the crushing grief that had driven her away in the first place.

The separation had changed her, not always for the better. She'd learned to compromise, to settle for less than what she really wanted, because she knew that life wasn't fair. But sometimes she'd settled for far too little, hadn't she? She'd let Matt get away with lies and betrayals that she should never have accepted. Maybe if she'd stood her ground with him more in the past, she wouldn't be in the mess she was in now.

But as her mother used to say, that was dirty water under

a rickety bridge. She had to deal with the here and now. And standing here in Wanda Langston's kitchen, surrounded by the people she loved most in the whole world, she felt like a whole new woman. In this place, she was no longer the woman Luke had known for almost a decade.

She was Abigail Jane Seymour, from Texarkana, and she was a force to be reckoned with.

She crossed back to Wanda, her drowsy son clinging to her side. "Wanda, this is my son, Stevie."

Wanda's eyes widened with surprise and no small amount of hurt, and Abby felt a rush of guilt for having stayed distant from Wanda and Billy for so long. "Good lord, Billy, did you hear that? Our Baby Abigail has a baby of her own."

"Hard to believe, ain't it?" Billy grinned. "I remember when you weren't any bigger than a pea pod, walkin' around here like you owned the whole world, and here you are a mama now."

"Now you're going to make me cry," Abby said with a watery chuckle. Stevie twisted in his arms to look up at her as if she'd grown an extra head. Had it really been that long since he'd heard her laugh?

"Are you staying here or are you just passin' through?" Wanda hurried back to the pot on the stove, which was threatening to boil over. "'Cause we've got plenty of room for the whole lot of you. Plenty to eat, too."

"We can't stay more than tonight," Luke said quietly. When everyone turned to look at him, he held his ground, though Abby thought he might have turned a shade redder at the sudden onslaught of scrutiny.

As Wanda opened her mouth to protest, Abby quickly backed Luke up. "It's a long story, Wanda. Billy can catch you up on it. Right now, though, we'll take you up on the offer of dinner and a place to stay. I've got to go change Stevie's diaper."

She made a quick escape into Wanda's small bathroom, just down the hall to the left. Closing the door behind her, she took a couple of deep breaths to push away the tears burning her throat and shook her head back, squaring her shoulders.

"Mama?" Stevie's voice was small and uncertain.

She stood him up on the counter, so that he was a head higher than she was. He looked down at her, catching her face between his small, grubby hands.

"It's okay, mister. You believe Mama, don't you?"

He just looked at her, his unusually solemn eyes reminding her of Luke's ability to see right through her.

"Let's get that wet diaper off, okay?" She picked him up again and swung him around to her back, where he clung like a monkey until she could fold a towel across the counter as a changing pad. She made quick work of the soiled diaper, remembering with wry annoyance that she'd planned to start Stevie on full-bore potty training this past weekend. That would have to wait, obviously.

She opened the bathroom door and almost ran into Luke, who stood on the other side, his hand raised to knock.

"Hey," he said, dropping his hand to his side.

"All done," she said with a smile. "I hope Wanda's got those turnip greens about ready, because I'm starving."

"You have an accent," he murmured, his gray eyes hooded.

"You can take a girl out of East Texas—"

"You didn't have it in California. Not like this, anyway."

She grinned up at him. "Well, your own accent is coming out to play a bit, too."

His lips curved slowly. "You're a bad influence."

"Or a good one," she countered, feeling wildly confident all of a sudden. Maybe it was as simple as being back home in Texarkana, where everything was familiar and real.

It had been a long time since she'd felt this way.

Luke's eyes narrowed even more. "Wanda said to meet her in Ross's old room and she'd help you get set up for the night." He stepped back to let her through the door.

She slid past him, not trying too hard to keep from brushing up against him as she passed. His soft intake of breath made her smile.

She'd gone a couple of steps down the hallway when Luke spoke behind her. "Nice homecoming picture, by the way."

She turned to look at him. "Wanda kept that picture, huh?"

"Seems she had hopes you'd come back home to Ross eventually. He's still not married, you know."

Was that jealousy glittering in Luke's gray eyes? "Wanda talks too much."

"It'll be hard for her to say goodbye to you again."

Abby hugged Stevie closer. "It'll be hard for me, too."

Luke walked down the hall toward her, his movements slow and deliberate. He cupped her cheek, his thumb moving lightly over her chin. "When this is all over, you should consider moving back here to Texas instead of staying in San Diego."

"Not as much linguistics work around here," she pointed out, her voice shaky because the idea was much more tempting than she'd expected.

"But you have friends here. People who'll watch out for you and Stevie. Everybody can use friends."

"How about you?"

He dropped his hand away from her face. His expression shuttered. "I'll be going back to San Diego when this is over."

"You may change your mind once you get home to Alabama."

He shook his head, stepping back toward the bathroom.

"I won't." He closed the door behind him, shutting her and Stevie out in the hallway.

*So much for feeling more confident,* she thought, trudging down the hallway toward Ross Langston's old room. She found Wanda inside, changing the sheets.

"There you are. I've just about got the bed made."

Abby set Stevie down on the floor and smiled at her old friend. "I can finish that. Shouldn't you be in the kitchen watching those turnip greens? My mouth is watering already."

"Billy's watching them. All done now, anyway—the corn bread will be out of the oven soon, and the ham'll take just a minute to warm up in the microwave." Wanda patted down the sheets. "If I'd known you were coming, I'd have fried up some crappie for you—Ross caught a limit last week on Wright Patman Lake. I know how you love fried fish and hush puppies."

Abby laughed. "Maybe it's a good thing I have to leave first thing in the morning. You'd pack ten pounds on my butt before the week was over with your cooking."

"Oh, I'd work it off you in the garden." Wanda gave her a hug. "Are you sure you can't stay? At least another day?"

"We can't stay," Luke said from the doorway.

At the sound of Luke's voice, Stevie toddled over to him, holding up his arms. Luke gave him an odd look, not moving immediately. Abby found herself holding her breath.

Then he bent and scooped Stevie up, tucking him close. "Hey there, scooter. You hungry as I am?"

"Take him on into the kitchen," Wanda suggested, putting her arm around Abby's waist. "We'll be right in."

Luke transferred Stevie to his hip and headed down the hall, pausing just a second to look back at Abby before he disappeared from view.

Wanda was quiet for a moment, her arm tightening slightly

around Abby's waist. Then she let go and turned to face her, her brown eyes warm with sympathy. "Does he know?"

Abby wasn't sure what Wanda was asking. "Know what?"

"That he's Stevie's daddy."

BILLY WASN'T IN the kitchen when Luke entered, but the sound of raised voices in the backyard made Luke's hair stand on end. Setting Stevie on one of the kitchen chairs and handing him a plastic napkin ring to play with, Luke crossed to the kitchen door and looked through the curtained pane.

Outside, Billy was arguing with a tall, rangy man wearing a police uniform. He had Wanda Langston's wiry build and Billy's dark hair and expressive face. *This must be their son, Ross,* Luke realized, watching the two men exchange urgent, heated words from his hiding place behind the curtains.

Great. Just great.

Abby's old boyfriend was a cop.

# Chapter Ten

"It's not what you think," Abby murmured.

"I don't really know *what* I think," Wanda replied gently. "Your husband's been gone for three years, so I don't reckon you were cheatin' on him or anything."

"It happened once, after Matt's death. Then Luke left for an overseas assignment and that was it." Abby winced inwardly. Maybe if it had been an affair that had ended the normal way, it would have been easier to deal with. But a one-night stand on the night of her husband's funeral? Humiliating.

She should probably hate him for it. But Luke had made no promises to her, nor she to him. And she didn't think there was anything that could make her hate Luke Cooper, anyway.

He was Stevie's father.

"Does he know?"

"I hadn't seen him since—no. He doesn't know he's Stevie's father," she answered.

The creak of floorboards just behind her sent a ripple of cold dread down her spine. She turned to find Luke standing in the doorway, Stevie perched on his hip. From the intensity of his gaze, she could tell that Luke had heard what she said.

He just didn't seem too surprised to hear it.

"Luke—" she started, swallowing a painful lump of dread that had lodged in her throat.

He shook his head, as if to dismiss an unwelcome subject. Instead, he turned to look at Wanda, his gaze accusatory. "You could have warned us that your son was a cop, Wanda."

Wanda looked surprised. "Is Ross here?"

"He's outside, arguing with Billy. Wonder why?" Luke's voice bit with sarcasm.

"Ross isn't going to cause trouble for Abby," Wanda said firmly. "You can depend on it."

"I can't depend on anything," Luke said darkly. "Abby, we have to get out of here. Now."

Abby understood Luke's concern, but Wanda was right. Ross Langston wouldn't hurt her. Not on purpose. And they could use all the help they could get. "Luke, it's okay. Ross may be able to help us. If nothing else, he'll know if the Texarkana Police Department receives an APB on us."

"I'd say they already have," Luke answered. "He and Billy were going at it pretty hard."

"I'll go see what's up. Y'all stay right here." Wanda patted Luke's arm on the way out. "And you stop worrying, you hear? He may be a grown man, but I'm still his mama. Ross won't be any trouble for you. I won't let it happen."

Luke watched her go, a furrow creasing his brow. "I think we should get out of here before Wanda has to test that theory."

Abby crossed to him and took Stevie, who leaned toward her with his arms outstretched, looking anxious. She kissed his forehead. "It's okay, baby. Everything's okay."

"I'm sorry." Luke made a move toward them with one hand, then seemed to think better of the gesture, dropping his arm back to his side. "I didn't mean to scare him."

"All this tension was bound to catch up with him," she answered. "He needs a little stability in his life again."

Sympathy tinged his voice. "I know."

"These people are the closest thing I have to family. Hell,

they *are* my family. All I have left. They're not going to do anything to hurt either of us. I know it as surely as you know you can trust your family to watch your back."

Luke didn't answer right away. His gaze was dark and intense, as if he was struggling to believe her. After a moment, he sagged against the door frame. "Okay. We'll stay put for now."

The sound of the back door opening sent a little shock wave through Abby's strung-out nervous system. She hugged Stevie closer and looked up at Luke, trying not to second-guess her trust in the Langstons. This was Texarkana, not San Diego, and unlike half the people she'd known over the past few years, Wanda, Billy and Ross didn't deal in secrets.

Maybe it was time to kick the habit of looking behind every smile for the lie it hid.

Billy entered the hallway, his expression calm. He flashed her a grin and a wink, and she felt more of the tension start to leave her body, unknotting the twist in her stomach. "We've got a dinner guest," he announced.

"We know," Luke said grimly.

Billy's expression fell at the open hostility in Luke's response. "Hell, son, I know y'all are in a mess of trouble, but you don't have to snap at me." He turned toward the kitchen. "Come on in here, Ross. The surprise is ruined."

Ross Langston stepped into the hallway. "Hey, Abby."

Despite the boulder-size lump in her stomach, she couldn't help but grin at his sheepish expression. "Hey, Ross."

He'd aged well, a few lines chiseled into his thin face, erasing the boyishness of his youth. He was taller than ever, lean but not lanky, with wide shoulders and strong-looking arms.

His grin widening, he picked up the pace, stopping in front of Abby with a look of familiar affection. "Hell, would you just look at you, Abigail Seymour. All grown up and prettier than ever." He tucked a twig of hair behind her ear, just as he'd used to do back when they were dating in high school.

"Sweet talker," she said with a grin. "So, still a policeman, huh? Never thought you'd last. You always liked trouble too much."

"You'd know. You got me into most of it."

"Liar."

Ross's grin faded, his brown eyes going serious. "Daddy says you're in a real mess. So tell me what you need me to do."

The offer, so simple and honest, hit Abby like a battering ram, breaking through her thin veneer of bravado. Overwhelmed by memories and a deep, abiding affection for her old friend, Abby flung herself into Ross's arms and started to cry.

"THE OTHER GIRLS on the dance team swore up and down that the chewing tobacco would make the bee sting stop hurting, and, well, you know Abby. She can't stand to see anybody in pain." Ross gave Abby a look of smitten affection that made Luke's blood go from a low simmer to a full-on boil.

"Hey, you were screaming like a little girl. I thought you were dyin', for Pete's sake." Abby's accent was in full drawl, Luke noted, and he'd never seen her look so relaxed or alive. He was really starting to hate Ross Langston now.

"How come you never told us this story back when it happened?" Wanda asked, mock censure in her motherly voice. Luke could see how happy she was to see Ross and Abby together again.

What woman wouldn't want her son to find a sweet, smart girl like Abby?

His own mother was going to love Abby once she met her. At least, she would if he could manage to drag Abby away from the Langstons and their stroll down memory lane long enough to remind her that scary bad men were hunting for them.

"So anyway, nobody warned me it was a bad, bad idea to swallow even a little of the tobacco juice," Abby said.

Despite his escalating annoyance with the happy reunion tableau spread out before him across the kitchen table, Luke had to wince with sympathy at the look of horrified memory on Abby's face. "Ugh."

She looked up with surprise, and Luke realized it was the first time he'd spoken since they sat down to dinner. "I thought I was going to throw up my liver." She shuddered.

"I was laughing so hard I forgot all about the bee sting," Ross said with a chuckle. "Poor thing turned green."

"You haven't touched your food," Wanda murmured to Luke. "I could fix you something else if you don't like this—"

He met her generous gaze and felt like a complete jerk. "No. This is great. I haven't had home cooking in a long time." He ate a bite of turnip greens and washed it down with treacle-sweet iced tea. It was all delicious and so familiar to him that it made his chest ache.

He needed to go home every bit as much as Abby needed to stay here in the warm and loving circle of her second family. But they couldn't separate. Not yet. Not until they found what Matt had taken and made sure Abby and Stevie were safe again.

*What about then?* a traitorous voice whispered in his head. *Can you really walk away from her and your son again?*

He clenched his jaw, forcing back the temptation. If Cordero ever found out the truth about Stevie—

He couldn't stay with her. End of discussion. Abby would understand, once he told her the whole truth.

She loved Stevie too much to risk his life for Luke.

He spent the rest of dinner avoiding her gaze, not yet ready to talk about the secret she'd revealed while talking to Wanda. But he felt her gaze fall on him several times, almost as tangible as a touch. He wondered whether she was hoping for a chance to talk to him about what he'd heard—or dreading it.

He finished his dinner, gave Wanda sincere praise for her cooking and gladly took up Ross Langston's suggestion that they go take a look around the property's perimeter to make sure nobody was lurking around. Abby might be hoping for a chance to talk, but Luke wasn't ready yet. Because he had a feeling that the truth wouldn't make Abby feel any better in the long run.

Outside, Ross lifted the collar of his uniform overcoat to ward off the cold breeze blowing in from the west and nodded for Luke to follow him down the slate-stone path toward the narrow lane that ran in front of Billy's house. "I don't reckon they've had a chance to figure out where you are yet, but it won't hurt to take a look-see."

"I guess Billy told you there's an APB out on the RV."

"Can't say I was happy to hear Dad's harboring a fugitive." Ross shrugged. "But Abby needs help, so we'll do it."

"I had a feeling you'd say that."

Ross looked sharply at him. "What's going on between the two of you? Are you together?"

Luke felt the unexpected urge to laugh. "Are you about to declare your intention to win her back or something?"

Ross glared at him. "No. That's over. Was before she ever left. But I care about her like family."

"Like a sister?" Luke asked softly, immediately feeling like a jerk. He had no right to feel jealous of Abby's relationship with Ross Langston, whatever it might have been.

"Close enough," Ross answered. "You got any sisters?"

"One."

"You'd do about anything to protect her, wouldn't you?"

Luke nodded. He'd already exiled himself from his family to protect all of them. There wasn't much he wouldn't do to keep Hannah and the rest of his family safe.

"Well, then you get where I'm coming from," Ross replied. "I'm just not as convinced as Daddy is that getting out of town is really what will keep Abby safe."

"You think you can protect her here?"

"Yeah, I do."

Luke sighed. If he really believed Abby would be safe here, he'd leave her and Stevie behind and pray that Cordero never got the chance to connect them to him.

"This'll be one of the first places folks look for her. Hell, we're taking a risk just staying here overnight." Luke shook his head, delivering his final assessment in terse, unyielding words. "We have to go first thing in the morning."

"Go where?"

"I can't tell you that."

Ross's eyes narrowed. "Because you don't trust me."

Trust wasn't the problem, Luke thought. He took Ross at his word, that he'd protect Abby with his life if necessary. But Luke believed the men who'd come here to question him and his family wouldn't be the type of people who'd accept a lie, even an earnest one, at face value.

And they'd have painful ways of getting to the truth.

"If you're lying to them, they'll know it. This way, you won't have to lie. You won't know where we went."

"I'll know what kind of car you're in."

"That won't matter." In a day or so, they'd be in Alabama. He could get Sam's help in ditching the borrowed car and finding another set of wheels. All he had to do was get to Alabama, and they'd be in a lot better shape.

"Okay," Ross said after a long, thoughtful pause. "I don't need to know where you're going or what you plan to do. But I'd kind of like to know where you've been."

Luke frowned, not following.

"How exactly do you know Abby? Where'd you meet?"

Luke wondered just how much Abby had told the Langstons about her life in San Diego. Despite his closeness to her, there was little about her life before California that Luke knew. She'd seemed to compartmentalize her life into "before Matt" and "after Matt." She hadn't talked about her past, beyond mentioning that her parents had died just after her graduation from high school. No talk of old boyfriends, old childhood memories—nothing that touched on her mysterious past.

Luke had often wondered if she'd had an unhappy childhood she'd been trying to escape. Now, he could see his speculation had been entirely wrong. It wasn't a tragic past that she had been hiding from. It was the tragic end to a happy one.

"I was her husband's friend," he answered Ross. "She became my friend when they married."

"I never met her husband." Ross's voice rang with regret. "Abby didn't write to me much after she went off to college, and I never visited her out there. I guess she missed her folks so much it was hard to have reminders of them. We would have been major reminders. Our families did everything together. Daddy was Mr. Seymour's right-hand man. We took vacations together, she and I went to school together—I always figured that's what she was really running from when she headed off to the other damned side of the country for college."

"Probably," Luke agreed.

"Was he good to her? Her husband?"

Luke wasn't sure how to answer. In many ways, he'd been a good husband to Abby—loving and attentive. He'd just never fully accepted the idea of fidelity. He liked to have fun, liked to scratch all his itches, and he'd never been much for deferring pleasure when it was there for the taking.

"He was good to her mostly," Luke answered carefully.

"Mostly?" Ross asked.

Luke shook his head. "If you want to know about Abby's marriage, you should talk to her. Not me."

"You're right." Ross sighed, digging his hands into the pockets of his jacket. They'd made it to the end of the Langstons' property, where it edged a narrow, burbling creek that glistened in the pale blue moonlight overhead.

It must have been a fun place to grow up, Luke thought, a little more flat and open than the hilly woods where he'd played out the boyhood dramas of his own childhood, but not so very different that he couldn't sympathize completely with Abby's clear desire to stay here and stop running.

She'd been running for a long time, more than just these past few days. So had he. And fugitives eventually reached the point where capture didn't seem as bad as running one more step.

Another thing he and Abby appeared to have in common.

"Let's head back in," Ross suggested.

Luke fell into step, deciding he liked Ross Langston after all. He seemed to be a solid, good-natured guy, and Luke believed him when he said that their secrets were safe with him, though he knew secrets always came out, one way or another.

Like the truth about Stevie's paternity.

With that secret now out in the open, it would be a race against time to make sure that particular truth didn't come back to haunt them all.

Abby was sitting in the faded rocking chair on the front porch, waiting for them to return. She smiled as they headed up the porch steps, but the tension in her eyes belied her friendly expression. Luke wasn't surprised when she told Ross to go on inside without her. "I need to talk to Luke in private."

Luke waited for Ross to close the door behind him before he

settled into the matching rocker next to Abby. He didn't turn his head to look at her. His stomach was in double knots.

"You must be so angry at me," she said. "I'm sorry."

He shook his head. "I deserve everything you must have thought about me after you woke up alone that morning."

"That doesn't change the fact that I had no right to keep the truth about your son from you."

Hearing her say the words—*your son*—sent pain ripping through his chest. Somehow, from her lips, the words sounded so real, so final. No more pretending he didn't know the truth.

Stevie was his son.

He bit his lip, fighting against the burning ache at the back of his eyes. "I understand why you kept it from me."

"I don't want you to understand!" Abby rose from the rocking chair and turned to face him. "Why aren't you angry at me? Do you even care that you have a son?"

He rose swiftly, startling her so much that she almost lost her footing. He caught her around the waist to keep her from falling. "Of course I care!" He tightened his grip on her, overcome by a flood of yearning so hard and deep that he thought he might drown if he had to let go of her. "It's everything I ever wanted but knew I'd never have."

In the yellow glow of the porch light, Abby's face glistened with falling tears. "Knew you'd never have?"

He forced himself to let go of her, not a bit surprised by the ripping sensation in his gut. It was an echo of the feeling that had overcome him that morning, almost three years ago, when he'd had to leave her bed and head for hell across the world.

He'd known then he could never come back to her.

Just as he knew, now, that what he had to tell her next would change everything between them forever.

"I can't be with you, Abby," he said softly.

"Is that what you think I want?" She lifted her chin, her eyes flashing with defiance. It would have been a convincing performance to almost anyone else in the world.

But Luke knew her better than almost anyone else. He'd seen her build walls around herself, slowly but surely, as Matt's distance and betrayals took their toll on her open, trusting soul. She'd gotten very good at pretending anger and indifference when she was hurting.

He'd hurt her badly by leaving. He knew because leaving her had been agony for him, a pain he'd relived every day since. He'd never really understood the meaning of the word *loneliness* until he'd looked into the bleak depths of a long, immutable future without her.

"I don't know what you want," he admitted. "I just know that no matter what I want, the outcome will always be the same. I can't be with you. I can't be Stevie's father."

The first crack appeared in her carefully-controlled facade, a faint tremble of her lower lip. She caught the traitorous lip between her teeth, pain seeping into the defiance in her bright blue eyes.

"Okay," she said after a moment. "He doesn't know any different anyway. He'll be okay."

Luke felt gut-punched at the thought of Stevie growing up without him around to experience it. "Abby, I need you to understand—"

"I understand," she said bluntly, pushing past him toward the front door.

He swung her around to face him. "No, you don't."

"We didn't make any promises," she said with a smile so forced that it was painful to see. "I know that. And I don't need child support or anything—"

"I can't acknowledge him because doing so would put a target on his back," Luke interrupted.

Her brow furrowed as his words worked their way past her

mental defenses. "A target? You think those guys following us will be even more ruthless if they know he's your son?"

Luke shook his head, hating to admit what he had to tell her now. "Abby, they're not the only people who are after us."

"Not the only—" She stopped short, her eyes darkening with understanding. "Oh, my God. The murder at the motel— that was someone else?"

He nodded.

"And they're after us?"

"Technically, after me," he said.

"Who? Why?"

Luke felt her shiver beneath his touch. He didn't think it was just from the cold night air. "Have you ever heard of Eladio Cordero?"

The furrow in her brow deepened. "The drug guy?"

He nodded.

"He's after you? Why?"

"Because four years ago, I killed his son," Luke answered.

## Chapter Eleven

The chill November night couldn't come close to matching the icy coldness that crept through Abby's body at Luke's confession.

Four years ago, he'd killed the son of one of the most brutal, elusive drug lords in the world. The kind of man who would never forgive such an act—or forget it.

And who had enough money and power to extend his brutal reach far beyond the confines of his hideout in the Sanselmo rain forest.

"How did that happen?" she asked aloud.

"It wasn't long after the coup attempt. Cordero had heavily funded *El Cambio* rebels to foment unrest among the labor unions and the farmers, for his own purposes, since the Morales government had begun seriously cracking down on marijuana and coca production in the rural areas. His own cartel put heavy pressure on the government through targeted assassinations and other strong-arm tactics."

Abby nodded, a little impatiently, because she knew the basics of what had happened during the uprising. She'd always made a point of keeping up with the news whenever Matt and Luke had been off on an assignment, trying to read between the lines of the few tidbits of information either of them had been able to share with her about their top-secret missions. "Was it connected to the Voices for Villages investigation?"

"We never found a direct connection between Cordero and the arms-for-drugs operation. But he does control a large segment of Sanselmo's drug trade, so it's possible."

"So maybe the people after us are connected to Cordero."

"Maybe. Except I think Cordero's men may have killed one of the operatives sent to find us. Why would they have done that if both parties were working together?"

She didn't know. Nothing was making much sense at the moment. "How did you kill Cordero's son?"

"We were ambushed. Matt and several of the others got away immediately. I was cornered and had to fight my way out. The last person between me and the rest of my unit was Tomás Cordero. He was one of his father's top lieutenants in the cartel. He'd been personally overseeing an attempt on the life of the president's son. We stopped him from succeeding, that time, anyway."

A later assassination had killed the president's eldest son, Abby remembered, another death added to the long list of assassinations and murders on Eladio Cordero's tab.

"You had to kill him to escape the ambush?" she asked.

Luke nodded. "A day later, I learned Eladio Cordero had already discovered who I was. He knew my name, my rank, everything that could be gleaned by public means and a few things I don't know how he learned without help from within our own government."

"A spy?" She stared at him, horrified. "In the Marines?"

He shrugged. "In the Marines, maybe. I don't want to think so, but you never know. Could also be in the armed services in general, or maybe even within the civilian government. Nobody's been able to tell me."

"Why would someone do that?"

"Money? I don't know. The information leak seemed to be a onetime thing, or, at least, I thought so until the murder in

Yuma. Cordero hasn't bothered me or my family. Not since—" He stopped short, looking away from her suddenly.

"Not since what?"

He sounded reluctant when he spoke. "I've never been a hundred percent sure that Matt's car crash was really an accident."

His words took a few seconds to sink in. When they did, Abby felt her dinner start to rise in her throat. She swallowed hard to combat the queasy sensation, trying to stay calm. "You think Cordero had Matt murdered? Why? Because Matt was your closest friend?"

"Matt wasn't my closest friend," Luke said softly. "You were. Matt was driving your car, remember?"

Abby sank into the rocking chair she'd vacated earlier, her legs too shaky to hold her. "You think it was an attempt on my life, not Matt's?"

"It could have been either, I suppose. Matt was a good driver. He wasn't drunk or impaired. He should have been able to handle that curve, even at the rate of speed he was going, if something else hadn't gone wrong."

"Why didn't you tell me your suspicions?" she asked.

He didn't answer, just sank into the rocking chair beside her, leaning forward with his hands clasped between his knees.

"Oh, my God." The events of those days after Matt's accident clicked into focus. So much of Luke's behavior that had confounded her at the time now made a horrible sort of sense. "That's why you didn't show up until the funeral."

"I was trying to find out more about the accident. I called in a lot of favors in order to be allowed to monitor the preliminary NCIS investigation." He slanted a look at her. "I needed to know if what happened was connected to Cordero."

"What if it was supposed to be you?" Her voice came out in a strangled croak. "Anybody who knew anything about you knew that you and I were friends. Maybe we both were the targets."

"He doesn't want to kill me," Luke said quietly. "He wants to punish me."

He was right, she realized. Eladio Cordero would never be satisfied by simply killing Luke. It wasn't his style, she knew. Some of her freelance translation work had involved a foundation dedicated to helping the victims of the Sanselmo drug wars. She'd heard tales of torment that had given her nightmares for weeks.

Cordero was famous for embracing Old Testament justice— an eye for an eye. Killing Luke wouldn't have seemed like fitting justice to a man like Eladio Cordero.

He would go after people Luke loved instead. Ruthlessly and efficiently.

"That's why you haven't been home in so long," she murmured. It all made sense now.

"The job kept me away for the first six years," he said. "I was bucking for promotions, working my tail off to rise in the ranks. I never took any time off then. But the last four years—yeah. That was why I stayed away from my family."

"How did you know he wouldn't go after them anyway?"

"I didn't. I tried to keep everybody out of it by just staying away, but Sam wouldn't let the situation stand. He flew out here a while back and wormed it out of me." Luke's grim smile made Abby's chest ache. "He started then and there keeping track of the latest information on Cordero—he had contacts inside the government and pulled every string he could find to stay informed. He had friends of his in the intelligence services keep an eye on *Los Tiburones*. That's what Cordero calls his enforcers."

"I know." She shuddered. She'd seen some of the scars that *Los Tiburones* had left on the bodies of their living victims.

"Sam also decided to move back to Alabama with his

daughter. Safety in numbers, I suppose. And he's there to watch out for the family." Luke passed a hand over his face. He looked as if he'd aged a decade in the past few minutes. "I don't know how long that's going to keep everyone safe. I've made such a mess of things."

"This isn't your fault."

"I should have tracked down Cordero before I ever left Sanselmo. I knew the kind of man he was. I knew he'd exact his revenge, one way or another."

"You're not a murderer," Abby said firmly.

"Maybe I should have been, that one time."

She didn't know how to argue against his point. If Cordero were dead, everything might be very different.

"I never should have stayed with you that night," Luke said bleakly. "I never should have dropped my guard and let things go so far between us. I knew better."

Because he'd already known about Cordero's vow of vengeance by then, Abby finished his thought silently.

Had that been the real reason he'd left without waking her? Why he'd stayed away since?

Was the truth as simple—and awful—as that?

She saw the answer in his eyes when she looked at him again. Something broke inside her, pouring equal parts pain and joy into her soul. "Oh, Luke."

"I'm sorry, Abby. I knew what I had to do would hurt you, but I didn't know any other way to keep you safe."

"And if you'd known about Stevie?"

"I'd have had twice the reason to stay away."

The bubble of joy she'd felt just moments earlier fled under the onslaught of dread. Stevie was Luke's son. Luke had killed Cordero's son.

An eye for an eye.

"Stevie," she said, her heart in her throat. "If Cordero learns he's your son—"

"Nobody else can know Stevie is my son," he growled.

She nodded, understanding everything now. "I know."

He turned the rocking chair to face her, pulling her around so that their knees touched. He caught her hands, folding them between his own. "I'm sorry, Abby. About everything. I can't tell you how sorry."

She pulled one of her hands free and lifted it to his face. His skin was cool, his unshaven beard beginning to grow thicker and longer. He looked tired and broken, and she didn't know whether to cry or to hold him.

She ended up doing both, pushing to her feet and pulling him up with her. She wrapped her arms around his waist and pressed her cheek against his chest, blinking back the hot tears spilling down her cheeks. "You kept us safe. There are no words to say how thankful I am for that."

He stroked her hair, his heartbeat loud and quick against her ear. For a second, she could almost forget that even this small moment of comfort between them could be as dangerous as standing in the middle of a battlefield without a stitch of armor. Feeling his fingers in her hair, his body warm and strong against hers, brought back memories she thought she'd excised long before.

"I missed you," he whispered against her temple. "Every single day."

She tightened her arms around him, afraid he was going to pull away. "I missed you, too."

He cradled her face between his hands and made her look up at him. "When you weren't cursing my name, that is."

She managed a smile. "Well, yeah. Except for then."

He stroked her cheeks with his thumbs. "Maybe we'll get lucky and Cordero will get hit by a truck."

"Or the Sanselmano government will get lucky with one of their raids," Abby suggested.

"A heart attack would work, too."

She chuckled again, wishing this moment of rare closeness between them wouldn't have to end.

But it would. All too soon.

"You're shivering," Luke said, wrapping his arms around her and holding her close again. "We should go inside."

"I don't want to," she protested. Inside, he'd let her go and they might never be able to hold each other again.

"We're going to go into hypothermia out here."

She released a little growl of frustration. "I'm not ready to let go yet."

"Just for a little while, Abs." He rubbed her back gently.

"You can't promise that," she whispered against his chest.

He was quiet a moment, his hand still moving slowly, soothingly against her spine. He finally let go, stepping back. "I can't promise anything. Except to do whatever I can to keep you and Stevie safe."

Even if that meant walking away, Abby thought.

She loved him for it, but she kind of hated him, too.

"Let's go say good-night to everybody," Luke suggested, giving her hand a gentle tug toward the door. "Then we'll talk after everyone's settled down for the night."

She tightened her grip on his hand, not budging. He turned back toward her, a quizzical look in his eyes.

"Not yet," she whispered, sliding her hand around the back of his neck and pulling him down to her until his mouth was inches away. Whether the fire coursing through her veins was born of the emotional roller coaster of the past few minutes or years of unrequited need, she didn't care. If ever there was a time for abandon, surely this moment was it.

She might never have the chance to touch him this way again. To say what needed to be said, so he'd know exactly where she stood. Where she'd always stood, even when she hadn't been free to tell him.

She slid her hand up to his jawline, running her thumb across his beautiful, tempting bottom lip. "I wasn't that drunk that night, Luke. I knew exactly what I was doing and what I wanted. And even now, knowing everything that's happened since, I don't regret it."

Luke stared at her as if she were crazy. But she also saw answering hunger in the murky depths of his eyes as he lifted his hands and cradled her face, his movements rough and reckless. He whirled her around, pressing her back against the rough pine clapboard of the front wall. The ridges of wood pressed into her back, the slight pain of contact immediately overwhelmed by a flood of fire consuming her, inch by inch.

She closed her fingers over his muscular forearms, holding him tightly just to keep from falling into a nerveless mass at his feet. Her breath caught in her lungs and burned there, making her feel light-headed.

"I regret it," he murmured, pressing his forehead to hers. "I regret the danger..." He nipped at the tendons of her neck, making her gasp aloud. "I regret—"

She silenced him, her mouth claiming his. Right now, she didn't care about regrets or consequences, not with Luke's body pressing hers into the wall, fiery-hot and demanding. He twined his fingers with hers and pinned her hands back against the rough clapboard, taking ruthless control of the kiss.

His tongue brushed over hers, lightly at first, then with relentless determination, until she was clinging to the last shredded edge of her control. He groaned against her lips, a feral growl of a sound that set off a rumbling sensation low in her belly.

With a sudden groan of frustration, Luke rolled away from her, coming to rest with his back pressed against the porch wall. "Stevie," he breathed, and that one word sent a cold shudder racing down Abby's spine, dropping her back into sober reality with a jarring thud.

"Stevie," she echoed, her stomach knotting with anxiety. How had she allowed herself to forget, even for a second, the threat Luke posed to her son by his mere presence? Stevie was her priority. He was Luke's priority. Keeping him safe was everything—the only thing—that mattered.

Luke reached over and touched her hand, a light brush of his fingertips against her knuckles. He dropped his hand back to his side and released a deep sigh. "You should go back inside now. I need a couple more minutes. I should touch base with Sam before we settle down for the night. He may have some ideas about where we should go next."

Abby nodded, even though the last thing she wanted to do was to go inside and face the Langstons at the moment. Surely the evidence of the searing kiss she and Luke had just shared was written all over her face, as if Luke had branded her irrevocably with his desire. She felt as if she were sixteen years old all over again, coming home from the junior prom, shaken and certain that her parents would see that she let Ross Langston get all the way to second base this time.

Maybe being back home in Texarkana wasn't as good for her as she'd thought. As much as she didn't like the woman she'd become in San Diego while living a lie of a marriage for six long years, she didn't want to revert to the scared little Texas girl who'd headed west for college with a head full of foolish dreams and naive notions about life that time and experience had knocked out of her one painful blow at a time.

"Go on," Luke said softly. "Stevie needs you."

She nodded. Stevie did need her. And she might be all he ever had, thanks to Eladio Cordero's vendetta.

She pushed away from the wall, waiting a second to see if her shaking legs would hold her before she took a faltering step toward the door. She stopped, turning back to look at Luke. "Can no one stop Cordero?"

"At least three different governments are trying," he answered in a dry, dark voice. "No luck so far."

Too many places to hide in the mountains and jungles of Sanselmo, she supposed, especially if you were filthy rich with drug money and surrounded by thugs whose lives you controlled.

She raked her fingers through her hair, trying to fix the mess Luke's hands had made. She supposed there wasn't much to do about the beard scratches on her throat and jaw, however.

"You look beautiful," he murmured.

She smiled, suddenly self-conscious. "I'm a mess. But thanks."

As she reached for the kitchen door, it flew open and Ross Langston stepped out onto the porch, almost running into her. He skidded to a stop, his eyes widening a bit as he took in their disheveled appearances. Even an idiot could have been able to figure out what had been going on between them seconds before. And Ross was no idiot.

But despite the slight flush of red that rose up his neck, his expression remained deadly serious. "I just got a call from the station. Someone called in a tip about your RV being at the dealership."

All the warmth that Luke's caresses had generated fled Abby's body. "How?" She'd been depending on at least a little lead time before they had to start worrying again. "Nobody even saw us. How could someone have found it so fast?"

"There are people looking for you. Apparently they're relentless," Ross answered. He looked at Luke. "Some detectives will be here soon. I've tried to stall them by asking to meet them at the dealership before they come over here to talk to Daddy about it. But the people who called in the tip may have been using the situation to find out where you'd go next. It won't be hard to figure out you came here."

"We have to go," Luke said quietly.

Ross nodded. "Mama and Daddy are inside packing you up for the drive. You're going to take Daddy's SUV and get out of here as soon as possible."

Abby's heart sank. She was tired, she was scared and the thought of getting into one more vehicle for one more overnight run for her life was enough to make her want to sit down right there on the porch and cry.

Ross caught her hand. "I'm sorry, Abby. I have to go."

She watched him leave, tears burning her eyes. When she looked at Luke, his eyes were dark with regret.

She couldn't stand there another moment or she'd root herself to the spot. No matter what her heart was whispering about home and safety, the only place she'd really be safe was with Luke.

They had to go.

Inside, she found Wanda in the kitchen, digging through the pantry for supplies to put into a large canvas bag. The look she gave Abby was full of love and fear, but Abby didn't have time to stop and reassure her that everything would be okay.

She needed to see her son.

She hurried down the hall to the bedroom and found Stevie still asleep, oblivious to the heightened tension in the house. He was beautiful in the sliver of light shining into the bedroom from the hallway, his eyes tightening a little as the light fell onto his face. He flopped his head over to block out the light and fell quickly into a deep sleep once more.

Tears burned her eyes, and she turned away, flattening her back against the hallway wall. Despair seeped into her bones, down to the marrow. As much as she'd needed to know the whole truth about why Luke had walked out on her three years ago, knowledge only increased her troubles tenfold. Now she knew she had two powerful, ruthless enemies who were willing to use her son's life as a bartering chip. And they were already here in Texas.

How was she going to keep Stevie safe now?

## Chapter Twelve

"Someone tipped off the Texarkana police," Luke said urgently into the disposable phone as he took the bags Billy handed him and shoved them into the hatch of the Dodge Nitro.

"This soon?" Sam asked, alarmed.

"We knew they'd be looking for us on the interstate routes. I guess they decided to branch out to the main arteries."

"You've got to get out of there."

"We're packing as we speak." He looked at Billy Langston, trying to convey his gratitude with his eyes. "I need to ditch these wheels soon. I'm going to need help from home."

"You've got it. I'll meet you halfway—"

"Shouldn't be you. They may be watching all the immediate family. Maybe Kristen?" Sam's wife, Kristen, was a cop. They could use the extra firepower, as well.

There was a brief pause while Sam murmured something to someone else—Kristen, apparently. Luke heard her quiet assent, then Sam said, "She's on her way. I'm giving her the spare disposable phone I bought the other day." He gave Luke the number. Luke dug in his jacket pocket for a pen and wrote the number on the back of his hand.

"Got it."

"Where do you want her to meet you?"

He looked at Billy, not willing to say in front of the other man. Billy read the reluctance in Luke's eyes and walked away, leaving Luke to pack the hatch by himself. "There's not a lot of point in subterfuge at this point," Luke said quietly. "I've been wondering why they tipped off the cops instead of coming here themselves. You can't tell me they don't know who the Langstons are to Abby. They had to know she might be here. I think they're herding us. Keeping us on the move."

"But they went after you in Yuma."

"Maybe *Los Tiburones* spooked them, so they're just tracking us, for now, to see if we've figured out where Matt hid whatever it was he took from them."

"You still have no idea what they're looking for?"

"I'm assuming he took incriminating files," Luke replied, glancing over his shoulder toward the Langstons' house. Where were Abby and Stevie? "There's something else you should know," he added quietly. "I told Abby the truth about Cordero."

Sam was silent for a moment. When he spoke, his voice was wary. "But you don't want to tell the rest of your family?"

Sam was right. It was time to trust his family to be able to take care of themselves. "Tell them," Luke said aloud. "Everything about Cordero. God willing, we'll be there in the next two days. They need to know what's coming their way."

"Are you sure?" Luke could hear the hope in Sam's voice.

"I should have told everyone a long time ago. They have a right to make their own choices about how to deal with it."

"Including Abby?"

Good question. What if he'd stayed there in her bed that morning and told her everything? She might have been willing to take her chances to be with him, but would he have let her risk it? Especially once Stevie was in the picture?

He had a feeling they'd have ended up in the exact same place they were now, even if he'd told her the truth.

"I don't think it would have made a difference. Neither one

of us is willing to put Stevie into more danger. We can't let anyone know he's my son."

"Not even the family?"

"Just you. And Kristen—I won't ask you to lie to her."

"Are you sure?"

An image of Stevie's mischievous grin flashed through Luke's mind, and his heart contracted. "I'm sure. Nobody else can know. I know they'd never let it slip intentionally, but—"

"I get it." Sam's voice softened a little on the other end of the line. "Does Stevie look like you?"

"Not obviously—he still looks more like Abby than anything. But, yeah. There's a resemblance." He heard the porch door creak open behind him and turned to see Abby coming, Stevie on one hip and his diaper bag in her other hand. Billy and Wanda were behind her, Billy carrying a large canvas tote brimming with groceries. "Sam, I've got to go. I'm heading west on Highway 82, toward Mississippi."

"Got it. Kristen will call with directions where to go next," Sam answered. "I love you, Luke."

Hot tears pricked Luke's eyes. "Love you, too, Sam." He rang off and turned to meet Abby's quizzical look. "Sam," he said, and turned toward the car, putting the last bag in the hatch to distract himself from the knot of emotion choking him.

While Abby buckled Stevie into the car seat Billy had already attached to the middle bench of the Dodge SUV, Billy gave Luke's arm a tug. Luke didn't like the stubborn set of the man's jaw.

"I don't think you should be taking her and her little boy tearin' across the country, runnin' from the police," Billy said when they were out of earshot.

"I can't leave her here."

"You're not just Abby's friend, are you?"

Luke glanced back at the car and found Abby watching him, a troubled look on her face. "It's complicated."

"She's going to get hurt, isn't she?"

He could lie to Billy, say everything would work out. But Billy wouldn't buy it. He'd respect the truth more. "I don't think there'll be any winners when this is all over, no."

"She should stay here with us, then."

Luke shot him a considering look. "You own, what? A shotgun? Maybe a crossbow for hunting?"

Billy gave him a black look. "And a bowie knife."

"Any military training?"

"Two years in the Texas Air National Guard." Billy sounded defensive. "Vietnam was over by then."

"What about Ross? Police-academy training doesn't count."

Billy pressed his lips into a tight line. "We're not the only ones willing to protect her. A lot of folks around here loved that girl and her family."

"You think Ross can convince the rest of the Texarkana Police Department to look the other way on the APB? And even if he can, are they going to lie to the state troopers? The Feds?"

Billy looked away.

"I've got five cops just in my immediate family," Luke said gently. "Two of my brothers are former military officers. So's my dad. We'll take good care of them both. I promise."

"For now, you mean."

"For as long as it takes to make them safe."

Billy looked over at Abby, his expression bleak. "Safe isn't the same thing as happy," he murmured.

No, it wasn't, Luke thought. But it was a hell of a lot better than dead.

THE GULFSTREAM V could hold as many as fourteen passengers, but only six men occupied the seats in the small jet, and of those, only Damon and Tris remained awake. The orders had come through three hours ago—rendezvous at the San Diego airport. Beckett, their team leader, would be waiting with instructions.

Beckett was one of the six passengers, a burly ex-drill sergeant with a weakness for cards and the ladies. Definitely not officer material in a conventional unit, which had annoyed more than one team member at the beginning of a career working for Barton Reid's personal army.

It hadn't taken long, however, to realize that despite his peccadilloes, Salvatore Beckett knew how to get things done, on time and under budget. And he didn't ask many questions, the virtue that perhaps appealed to Barton Reid the most.

"Cooper hasn't been home in ten years," Tris murmured to Damon across the narrow space between their seats, which faced each other near the back of the Gulfstream. They had managed to get seats away from the others, all men from the East Coast office of MacLear Enterprises who'd traveled west a couple of days earlier to help in the search for Abby Chandler. "What makes the boss think he's heading there now?"

"He's heading *somewhere*. Home seems as good a bet as any." Damon tried not to look interested. Like all the members of MacLear's Special Services Unit, Damon had won his job by his personal vulnerabilities as well as his special skills. The vulnerabilities gave MacLear ammunition to use against him. His skills made his vulnerabilities an acceptable risk.

The fatal flaw that had put Damon in MacLear's crosshairs had been a very public taste for the finer things in life, far beyond his ability to pay for them. His personal debt had reached six figures when he was recruited eight months ago, trading one debt for another.

Tris's gaze settled on the four men sitting closer to the front of the jet. He didn't trust them. Neither did Damon. Lack of trust was one of the downsides of the Special Services Unit. Camaraderie was limited to the handful of men you worked with day in and day out. The sort of service-wide pride and honor typical of military units was missing entirely.

A shame, really. All the men in the Special Services Unit were talented, intelligent operatives. If not for their personal flaws, they could have made a damn fine unit for a company working aboveboard.

On the surface, MacLear was a legitimate global security firm, with offices located in Los Angeles, New York, Chicago, Atlanta and Miami, plus foreign offices in London, Berlin, Tel Aviv and Jakarta. They specialized in corporate security and threat risk assessment and training for businessmen working in foreign cities. Their CEO, Jackson Melville, was one of the cable news networks' go-to guys for security analysis when anything went wrong anywhere in the world.

He was also bought and paid for by Barton Reid, the number-three man in the State Department. When Reid needed something done quietly and ruthlessly, he turned to MacLear.

Neither Damon nor his fellow operatives could have proven the connection in a court of law. Reid had made sure of that. But it was an open secret that Barton Reid was involved in the company up to his neatly shaped eyebrows.

"Cooper knows we'll have his home covered," Tris said.

Damon had a feeling Cooper didn't care. The man had five brothers—one a sheriff's deputy, two auxiliary deputies, another who was a former Marine and his eldest a retired Navy lieutenant. His sister was married to another deputy, and his father had been a Marine sharpshooter in Vietnam. Maybe Cooper figured he'd be safer holed up with his well-armed family than wandering around alone with a woman and a baby in tow.

"I knew we were going to have trouble as soon as Mrs. Chandler went to Cooper's place," Tris added softly. "I could tell by looking at him that he'd be wicked trouble."

"Do you think he has what we're looking for?"

"Hell if I know," Tris answered.

Damon leaned back in the seat, closing his eyes and feigning sleep. He was tired of listening to Tris's complaints. The man had sold his soul to MacLear and Barton Reid willingly enough. Like all of them in the Special Services Unit, he could have chosen a harder but more honorable way out of his troubles.

Damon had no idea what was waiting in Alabama or how ugly the situation would get before it was all over. He hadn't even had a chance to think about what going back to his own home state for the first time in years would feel like.

Right now, he didn't have the luxury of caring. He had a job to do. If he failed, a lot of people would suffer for it.

He couldn't afford to let that happen.

ABBY HAD EXPECTED STEVIE to sleep for most of the night, as he had for the past two nights of driving. But he woke around 10:00 p.m. crying. Fortunately, Luke had taken the wheel for the first leg of the drive, which freed Abby to deal with her cranky son. She'd had the forethought to sit on the bench seat beside Stevie instead of up front in the passenger seat, putting her in a better position from which to cajole him into a happier mood.

"How about I tell you a bedtime story?" she suggested, giving Stevie a little nudge. "You love the Silly Squirrel story, don't you?"

Stevie glared at her, his eyes looking a little glassy in the dim light of the highway lamps. Alarmed, she pressed the back of her hand to his forehead. He felt hotter than usual.

"Luke, can you turn on the dome light a second?"

"What's wrong?" Luke asked, doing as she asked.

Abby met his gaze in the rearview mirror. "He feels a little warm. He may be coming down with something."

"Is it serious?"

She checked Stevie over, looking for signs of a rash or anything else that could clue her in to what was wrong with her son. She nudged Stevie's mouth open, but he clamped it shut and started to cry. "Come on, baby, Mama needs to look at your teeth. Pretty please?"

He relented, still sniveling, and she saw some redness in the back of his right gum. "He could be cutting one of his second molars. I need to get some stuff from the bag stored in the back hatch." She looked outside, peering past the glare left by the dome light, and saw that they had just hit the outskirts of a town. Ahead, she saw the darkened facade of a strip shopping center, already closed down at this time of night. "Can we pull over at that shopping center for a minute?"

Luke took a right at the light and pulled into the parking lot, nosing the car into a slot as far from the road as possible. He turned to look at Abby. "Are you sure he's okay?"

He looked worried, Abby thought, feeling a little sorry for him. She'd had two years to get used to figuring out which of Stevie's occasional illnesses required quick medical attention and which required patience and a little motherly coddling. She was pretty sure it was teething that was causing him to run a low fever. A teaspoon of liquid baby analgesic and some numbing ointment on his gums should do the trick.

"Just teething," she reassured him. "I have everything he needs in the smaller bag in the back. Can you get it for me?"

Luke retrieved the bag from the back hatch, bringing it around to the side door where Abby sat. He hovered as she dug through the bag and found the medicines she needed. As she'd hoped, Stevie settled down quickly after she applied the numbing ointment to his tender gums, cuddling close as she soothed him with a soft, slightly off-key lullaby. He was back to sleep in a few minutes.

"How'd you do this by yourself?" Luke's expression still betrayed anxiety. "I'd have freaked the first time he sneezed."

"Oh, I did all that. Drove him to the emergency room the first time he scratched himself and drew blood." Her first year as a mother had been an exercise in fear and paranoia. For a while, every cough had been pneumonia, every rash the measles, every bump and bruise a life-or-death crisis. Thank God for a patient, understanding pediatrician, who'd helped her through the panic attacks and the bouts of self-doubt. She and Stevie had made it through just fine, and he was a healthy, well-adjusted boy of two despite her doubts and inexperience.

"You would have been fine," she told Luke, catching his hand and squeezing it. "You'd have panicked the first few times you were left alone with him, maybe, but you'd have finally figured out, like I did, that babies are pretty hardy little creatures. They have to be, to survive life."

"I wish I could have been there."

She wondered if he was angry with her for keeping Stevie's existence a secret, now that he'd had more time to think about it. She couldn't blame him if he was. "I should have told you, Luke. It was all just so crazy at the time. Letting people believe Matt was his father was easier. I was a coward."

"You were a survivor." He ran his thumb over the back of her hand. "Probably saved his life by keeping his relationship to me secret."

She sighed, frustrated all over again. She'd spent the past few hours going over and over in her mind all that Luke had told her about Eladio Cordero's vendetta against him. Was there really no way to thwart the man's vengeance? Witness protection, maybe? Some other way to stay under Cordero's radar permanently?

The thought of walking away from Luke again was so disheartening she felt like crying.

But she didn't have time to cry. They had an even more pressing problem to cope with than Eladio Cordero. Somehow, they were going to have to figure out what Matt had stolen and where he'd hidden it, before their black-clad pursuers finally tracked them down, as daunting a task to Abby as figuring a way out from under Cordero's threats.

With Stevie fast asleep again, Abby climbed into the front passenger seat. She looked over at Luke, who was still looking back at Stevie, his brow furrowed with anxiety. "He's okay, Luke. I promise."

Luke looked over at her, flashing a sheepish smile. "He's a great kid, isn't he? You've done such a good job with him."

She smiled, though her heart ached at the eagerness in his voice. Luke kept swearing he didn't blame her for keeping Stevie's paternity a secret, but she didn't see how it could be true. If someone had kept her son from her for two years, she'd have been out for blood. "He reminds me of you all the time."

Luke's smile widened. "Yeah?"

"Yeah." She grinned. "He loves horses and hates carrots."

Luke chuckled. "Yeah? Well, what's his position on heavy metal, fishing with live bait and the designated hitter?"

"Get back to me in a few years and I'll let you know." As soon as the words slipped past her lips, she knew she'd said the wrong thing. Luke's smile faded quickly and his grip on the steering wheel tightened.

*Way to go, Abby. Remind him again that he's not going to be part of his son's life.*

Several minutes passed in silence, broken only by the

occasional rumble of a passing car on the highway. Finally, Abby couldn't stand the quiet any longer. "I wonder when your sister-in-law is going to call."

"Soon, I think." Luke's gaze dropped to the dashboard clock, which read 10:43 in glowing blue numbers. They'd been on the road for over three hours.

"Then what?" she asked.

After a brief pause, Luke answered, "I've been giving that a lot of thought. Going back over the time between our last stint in Sanselmo and the day of Matt's death. If he got his hands on any sort of damning evidence against Voices for Villages, it would have had to have been during that tour of duty. Before that, we didn't have a notion that the organization might have been doing anything illegal."

"Could Matt's relationship with that woman have been an assignment? Would you have known?"

"I led that investigation, so yeah. I'd have known." He sounded apologetic. "Although it's possible he chose not to end it with Janis Meeks when I told him to because he was trying to do a little undercover work of his own, I suppose."

That sounded like Matt, she had to concede. The job was his real mistress, and a lover was no more likely than a wife to sway his true devotion to it. "Okay, maybe we should look at this problem another way. What kind of evidence could he have gotten his hands on by playing this Meeks woman? What would drive these people to take so many risks and make so many threats to find it?" She turned in the seat to look at him, feeling the chaos of unanswered questions begin to coalesce in her mind and shape itself into patterns. "These people are putting a lot on the line to get to us, aren't they?"

"Yeah, I'd say so," Luke agreed. "So they must have serious money to burn."

"And a good reason to burn it," Abby said. "So whatever

Matt took, it must be huge. The guy from Boston said it was files, right?"

"I think he was guessing," Luke cautioned.

"But it makes sense. Files are about the only thing that would be incriminating enough to merit the kind of full-court press we're getting from these people." Abby's mind was clicking on all cylinders finally, filling her with a fresh sense of purpose she'd come damned near to losing just a few hours earlier. "Physical files?"

Luke shook his head. "Too bulky, too hard to hide—" He stopped short, his eyes widening suddenly with realization. "Son of a bitch."

"What?" she asked eagerly.

"I'm not a hundred-percent sure what Matt took," Luke answered, a smile spreading across his face, "but I have a damned good idea where he hid it."

# Chapter Thirteen

The Gulfstream V had landed at Birmingham-Shuttleworth International Airport at around 11:00 p.m. A tall, thin man dressed in a golf shirt and a crisply ironed pair of khaki chinos greeted them on the tarmac with a stack of file folders, which he gave to Beckett to pass out to the rest of the team while the man in the chinos introduced himself as Davenport from the Atlanta office and began barking out a quick summary of what they'd find inside.

"Tris, Damon, Malcolm—you're headed straight to Chickasaw County to stake out the Cooper Cove Marina. You have rooms booked at the Sycamore Inn, and someone has already checked in for you." He handed out room keys. "Go straight to your rooms and get a good night's sleep. Damon, you're booked for a fishing trip with Hannah Patterson at 6:00 a.m." He waved toward the hangar where the Gulfstream was being parked as he spoke. "The red Camry is yours. Key's in the ignition."

Relieved to be going solo for this leg of the assignment, Damon followed directions to where the Camry was waiting inside the hangar. When he cranked the Camry's engine, a man in gray coveralls waved him forward, and he drove out of the hangar and onto the service road that led out of the airport. He found the on-ramp to I-59 and headed onto the interstate highway, a flood of familiarity washing over him as he briefly spotted the sprawling Birmingham skyline to the southwest before he headed in the opposite direction, away from town.

Within an hour, he was well out of town, heading north into the Appalachian foothills dotting the northeastern corner of the state. No worry about directions; the map to his destination had already been stored in the Camry's built-in GPS.

MacLear thought of everything.

Knowing just how thorough MacLear could be, Damon had come prepared. He pulled a small electronic device from his pocket and pushed the center button. A few small lights flashed in the dark interior of the Camry.

No bugs. He released his pent-up breath and pocketed the device again, sliding it back into the hidden pouch inside his windbreaker pocket. Dropping his hand to his hip, he pulled out another device he'd secreted inside a second hidden pocket. Unlike his official MacLear satellite phone, this little piece of comm gear would not be monitored.

There was only one number programmed into the mini-phone, and Damon knew he had to press the button five times before the call would go through. Even then, when a careful male voice answered, Damon had to recite a sixteen-character password, consisting of both numbers and letters—a code that changed weekly based on a predetermined set of parameters that only two people in the world knew. Damon was one of them. The man who finally took his call was the other.

"Where are you?" Alexander Quinn asked tersely.

"Home," Damon answered. "Or just northeast of there."

"So you were assigned to the mop-up." Quinn sounded unsurprised. He'd predicted the assignment when Damon had talked to him before boarding the Gulfstream in San Diego.

"Smug it up, will you?"

Quinn laughed softly. "I've done a little more looking into Cooper's background. Resourceful fellow, Major Cooper.

Won't be as easy to bring in as your MacLear friends believe. He'll make it to Gossamer Ridge if that's where he wants to be."

"If that's where he wants to be," Damon echoed, checking his rearview mirror to make sure no other vehicles were sticking close to him. Tris and Malcolm had been well behind him, so he didn't have to worry about their sticking close, but he knew the people who ran MacLear weren't exactly the trusting sort. Every day he had to worry about his hidden agenda being exposed.

If the people at MacLear ever figured out his secret, Damon wasn't sure even Quinn would be able to help him.

"You're close, Damon. I can feel it." The excitement in Quinn's normally calm voice sent a little rush of adrenaline pouring into Damon's system. He knew finding the information Matt Chandler had apparently squirreled away could bring down MacLear and Reid. It was the Holy Grail, and Quinn had given Damon the honor of being the man best positioned to find it.

He'd do his damnedest to live up to Quinn's faith in him.

He rang off and concentrated on the darkened highway ahead, going over his plan for the next day as he drove. Their background on the sister, Hannah Patterson, suggested she was smart and outgoing. Liked to talk.

He might be able to use her extroversion to his advantage.

"I DIDN'T MAKE the connection before, but I should have. The office scanner spent long enough 'in the shop' to draw the attention of the company master." In front of Luke, the highway stretched out, flat and expansive. Crossett, Arkansas, was a faint glow in the rearview mirror, and Hamburg lay about twenty minutes to the northeast. They would stay on Highway 82 all the way to Starkville, Mississippi—unless Kristen called between now and then with different instructions.

"You think Matt somehow faked the scanner malfunction?" Abby sounded thoughtful, not skeptical. After a moment, she nodded. "Yeah, I could see that. He spent a lot of time in his garage workshop in the days before the crash." Her voice darkened. "By then, I'd stopped trying to figure out what he was up to. I knew I probably didn't really want to know."

"If he was scanning the files, the point was to digitize them, right?" Luke continued.

"So we're looking for—what? A DVD? A flash drive?"

"A USB flash drive," Luke said, almost certain he was right. "A few weeks before we deployed to Sanselmo, several of us in the unit pooled our money and bought a bunch of large-capacity flash drives in bulk. We split the drives among us to store photos to send home to our families." He smiled, but it felt a little bittersweet. "Some guys didn't make it back, so we were tasked with making sure their families got the last photos they took."

"And you think Matt stored the scans of the files he stole on one of those flash drives?"

"Yes."

"So where is it now?"

Luke glanced at her. "I think—I hope—it's somewhere at my parents' house in Gossamer Ridge."

Abby looked puzzled. "How would it have gotten *there?*"

"The day I mailed the disks home, I was called into an emergency meeting. Matt offered to post the package for me."

"And you think he put an extra disk into the package?"

"I called my mom to make sure she got the disks. She did, but one of the disks seemed to have some sort of strange encryption. They couldn't open that one."

"And you didn't think that was odd?"

"My parents aren't exactly computer whizzes. They handed it off to Hannah, I think. She's like a bulldog—she's probably still trying to get the damned thing to open." He chuckled.

Abby went quiet. He slanted another quick look her way and found her staring at the darkened highway, her brow furrowed.

"What is it?" he asked.

"I knew so little about Matt, didn't I?" She sighed. "I wonder if he even loved me."

"He loved you as much as he knew how," Luke said gently. "He just wasn't cut out for marriage. He shouldn't have tried."

"I was so alone when I met him. I wanted my family back, and he was funny and sweet and swept me off my feet." Tenderness, tinged with regret, resonated in her voice. "I should have waited. Been more sure."

"I think everything happens for a reason."

She chuckled softly. "Even bad marriages?"

A trilling sound set his nerves jangling. He reached into his jacket pocket and pulled out the disposable phone. "Yeah?"

A woman answered. "Luke, it's Kristen. Sam's wife."

He smiled bleakly at her self-introduction. She and Sam had been together for nearly a year now, and this was maybe the third or fourth time they'd even spoken. "Long time, no talk."

"How are y'all doing?"

"Hanging in there. Sam said you'd have instructions."

"I'm somewhere around Starkville. Where are y'all?"

"Nearing Hamburg, Arkansas, on Highway 82."

"Okay, good. Stay on 82 all the way into Greenwood, Mississippi. I should get there first, so I'll book a room at a motel and call with directions." Kristen's no-nonsense tone reminded Luke of a gunnery sergeant he'd known. The whole world around them could be going to hell and Gunny'd had a way of keeping them focused on the mission, one step at a time.

His sister-in-law would have made a good Marine.

"All right, we'll keep heading east and wait for your call." Luke rang off and told Abby what Kristen had said.

"A real bed?" Abby asked softly. "With a real bathroom?"

He smiled in sympathy. He'd grown to loathe the bathrooms in fast-food restaurants himself during their road trip. "That's the plan."

Abby leaned back against the headrest and closed her eyes. "Three more hours," she whispered, almost like a prayer.

*Three more hours,* Luke echoed silently.

Then the hard part would begin.

THE BUDGET ARMS in Yuma had sported a certain kitschy desert charm compared to the Motel 82 in Greenwood, a converted two-story brick apartment complex left to fend for itself in the hot Mississippi sun. The motel-room doors had once been painted a happy sky blue, but the paint had long since faded to a sad muddy aqua, underlining the dilapidated state of the grimy masonry and dented aluminum awnings.

The neon sign over the motel office was mostly dim, the *2* in *82* feebly flickering a sickly yellow every few seconds before subsiding into darkness again. As Luke parked the Dodge in front of one of the rooms, Abby stared out the window at the hapless sign and sighed, wondering what the Cooper family had against a halfway-decent budget motel.

"You're killing all the roaches," she murmured to Luke.

"This one's not my fault."

"You're still killing all the roaches."

The dashboard clock read 2:20 a.m. Almost an hour ago, Kristen had called Luke back and given him directions to the motel, telling him to park in front of room 1C, unpack everything from the SUV and knock on the door.

"Can we trust her?" Abby asked. "I mean, I know she's your sister-in-law, but she's also a police officer—"

"With no jurisdiction in Greenwood."

"She could be setting up a trap for the locals—"

"No," Luke said firmly. "She's a Cooper."

"You thought Ross was setting us up," she grumbled as she unbuckled her seat belt and opened the car door.

"Yeah, but he was your ex-boyfriend. Completely different dynamic." Luke shot a grin her way as he opened his own door.

He got the bags while Abby unbuckled Stevie from the car seat. The little boy cried a little until his face settled into the curve of her neck, then settled down and went back to sleep.

"I'll get the car seat in a minute." Luke came around the SUV with their bags. He nodded toward the motel-room door.

Abby knocked on the sad blue door. She heard the faint sound of movement inside, then everything went silent. She glanced at Luke, who shrugged at her.

The door opened suddenly, revealing a slim blonde dressed in jeans and a light green sweater. Her long hair was pulled back into a severe ponytail, which would have been a terrible look for a lot of women, but it worked for the blonde. She had clear blue eyes and a kittenish face, with wide cheekbones and a small, pointed chin.

The woman's gaze briefly took in Abby and Stevie before settling on Luke, a smile playing over her lips. "I suggested Sam give us code words to use," she drawled, "but hell, you're all Cooper. No mistaking that. I'm Kristen."

Luke grinned at the blonde. "I'm Luke. This is Abby and her son, Stevie. You gonna let us in, sis?"

Her smile widened and she stepped back to let them inside the small motel room. There was only one bed, Abby noted with chagrin, and the bedspread had seen better days.

Much better days.

"I wouldn't touch that bed," Kristen warned. "Sit in the chair by the desk. We're not going to be here long."

"We're not?" Abby asked, not hiding her relief.

"This is for show." Kristen's eyes took in the bags Luke had dropped on the floor just inside the room. "Where's Stevie's car seat?"

"In the SUV," Luke answered.

"Get it on the way out," Kristen said briskly. She handed Luke a set of keys. "The blue Jeep Cherokee three slots down. Bags in the trunk, then set up the car seat in the back. I've got to make a quick call and I'll be right out."

Rising wearily from the desk chair, Abby followed Luke outside the motel room and into the cold November night. "She's not much for the niceties, is she?"

Luke grinned as he stopped at the Dodge to fetch the car seat. "I like her."

"Yeah, 'cause she reminds you of a drill sergeant."

He shouldered the car seat and followed her to the dark blue Jeep parked three slots down, just as Kristen had said. He set up the car seat first, so Abby could belt Stevie in while he was stashing the bags in the trunk.

Abby yawned as she finished buckling her son in. "Who's she calling, your brother?"

"I guess so." Luke came up behind her, sliding his hands over her shoulders. She leaned back against him, grateful for his warmth and strength. "How're you holding up?" he asked.

"I was kind of hoping to sleep in a bed tonight, but not the one in there." She nodded toward the motel room. "I guess she must have booked the room for a couple of nights so nobody will think the SUV's been abandoned?"

"Probably." He bent his head, pressing his cheek to hers. He'd shaved at the Pattersons', but they hadn't had time for baths or much else since then, and his beard was growing thick.

She smiled at the bristly tickle. "Maybe she's booked a nicer hotel room somewhere. With a big tub."

His voice rumbled against her neck. "And clean sheets."

"Maybe those yummy mints on the pillows—"

Kristen emerged from the motel room, tucking her cell phone into the front pocket of her jeans. She walked quickly to the Jeep and looked over the roof at them. "Y'all set?"

Luke opened the front passenger door for Abby. "I'll sit back here with Little Bit."

Abby glanced at Stevie, reassuring herself that he wasn't fussing. He was sleeping peacefully in his car seat.

Poor baby. He'd been a trooper for almost the whole trip, not fussing too much when she'd had to change his diapers on public diaper tables in fast-food joints or buckle him back into his car seat when he should have been cuddled up in his crib.

"Please tell me we're going to a nice motel for the night," she murmured when Kristen slid behind the steering wheel.

Kristen gave her an enigmatic look but didn't answer. Abby looked over her shoulder at Luke, who was buckling in next to Stevie's car seat. He gave a little shrug.

Kristen drove the Jeep back onto Highway 82, heading back to the west, from where they'd come. Abby gave Luke another questioning look.

"Aren't we going the wrong way?" Luke asked.

Kristen shook her head. "We're heading to the airport."

Luke frowned. "Why?"

"Because that's where the bird is waiting." Kristen turned

off the highway onto a two-lane road that wound about a quarter mile through a wooded buffer zone before the runways of Greenwood-Leflore Airport came into view. She bypassed the terminal, slowing only when they were past the main runways. She turned the Jeep down a narrow lane near the western perimeter of the airport. The lane ended in a large Quonset hut set well apart from the rest of the airport structures. A dark blue helicopter sat quietly on a flat square strip a few yards from the metal building.

"We're flying in that?" Luke asked.

Kristen cut the engine and opened her car door. "You'll be in Gossamer Ridge by morning." Not waiting for them to join her, she exited the Jeep and headed for the Quonset hut.

Abby looked back at Luke. "You still like her?"

Not answering, Luke got out of the car, turning back to retrieve Stevie from his car seat. Stevie woke this time and started crying for Abby.

"Shh, baby." She took him from Luke's arms. "I hope your family knows what they're doing."

"Me, too," Luke murmured, quickly unlatching the seat and swinging it over his shoulder. He went around to the back, put the car seat down on the ground and checked the hatch. It opened and he started pulling the bags out of the back.

Movement near the Quonset hut drew Abby's attention. She saw Kristen walking back toward them, accompanied by two men. With only moon glow and the distant lights of the airport illuminating them, Abby could make out only a few details. Both men had short dark hair and were dressed in jackets and jeans. From a distance, they reminded her of Luke.

"Luke," she said.

Luke looked up at her, following her gaze to the approaching trio. He released a soft profanity and dropped the bags by the car. He took a couple of unsteady steps toward Kristen and the newcomers before picking up his pace, reaching Kristen and the unidentified men at a near-run. Abby tightened her grip on Stevie and followed.

Luke skidded to a stop in front of the shorter man, who grabbed Luke's upper arms tightly in both hands. He flashed a smile that gleamed white in the moonlight, then pulled Luke into a fierce bear hug.

Shocked by the sight of Luke Cooper with his face buried in the other man's neck, his shoulders shaking with unmistakable emotion, Abby faltered to a halt a few steps away, her heart pounding a frantic, unsettled cadence.

Kristen left the men and came to Abby's side. "It's okay," she said, reaching up and rubbing her hand against Abby's back in a soothing circle. "He's okay."

At the sound of Kristen's voice, Luke pulled away from the shorter man and turned to look at Abby, his face damp with tears. He shot her a watery smile and reached out his hand to her.

She walked to his side, her gaze locked with his. Only when one of the other men spoke did she drag her attention away from Luke's emotion-racked face.

"You must be Abby. And this is Stevie?"

Abby looked up at the second of the two strangers, who stood a couple of steps behind the man who'd hugged Luke earlier. He looked to be in his early forties, with short black hair flecked with silver and pale eyes that betrayed perpetual sadness, despite his welcoming smile.

"This is my oldest brother, J.D.," Luke said, his voice thick and unsteady. "Former Navy mechanic and helo pilot."

"Flew a Seasprite," J.D. said, still smiling. Still looking sad, somehow. Then Abby remembered. J.D. was the one whose wife had been murdered. Luke had told her J.D. still wasn't really over it.

"And this is Sam." Kristen walked to the other man's side

and slid her arm around his waist. Her earlier no-nonsense demeanor melted into a look of sheer adoration as she gazed up into her husband's happy face.

"Nice to meet you, Abby." Sam smiled at her, his gaze sliding down to take in Stevie, as well. Something in his expression shifted, and Abby realized Sam knew the truth about her son. She looked up at Luke, who put his arm around her and grinned, looking younger and happier than she'd ever seen him.

"J.D.'s going to fly us back to Gossamer Ridge," he said, his voice bright with excitement. "We're going home."

# Chapter Fourteen

There was no one else in the Quonset hut when Sam and J.D. led them inside. The interior was full of supplies, helicopter parts and, near the far end of the structure, two helicopters sheltering from the cold within the building's cavernous belly.

"The guy who runs this hangar finished refueling us, and he's gone back home for the night. We're supposed to padlock the place when we leave," J.D. explained.

"Mighty trusting," Abby murmured.

"He's the brother of the guy who owns that chopper out there. You remember Barry Rutledge, don't you, Luke? The guy who runs Chickasaw County Aviation." J.D. walked ahead to a narrow, podiumlike desk near the side door of the hut and started writing something on a sheaf of papers attached to a clipboard.

"Why don't we go get Stevie's car seat set up in the helicopter?" Kristen suggested to Abby, giving her a light nudge toward the open hangar door.

"We'll be right behind you." Sam waited for them to get out of earshot before turning to Luke. "You hanging in there?"

Luke felt another sting of tears burning the back of his eyes. "Yeah. It's just—"

"Complicated?" Sam suggested.

Luke smiled. "I do seem to be using that term a lot these days. Listen—anything new on either Reid or Cordero?"

"Not on Reid. On Cordero, I'm hoping some queries I've made will pan out soon."

"Half the democracies in the western hemisphere are looking for Cordero. If they can't get their hands on him—"

"I'm hearing really good things about the new president of Sanselmo. People I trust tell me Almovar is dead serious about cleaning up the cartels. He's putting a lot of political capital on the line to stop Cordero and his cohort."

"And painting a target on his own back," Luke added bleakly. "I wonder what Barton Reid thinks of him."

"Reid's buddies in the region loathe Almovar. They don't trust his good relationship with the United States. So my guess is, Reid is probably looking for ways to undermine Almovar."

"And help Cordero," Luke added. "What if Reid and Cordero have joined forces to find Abby and me?"

"You should have told us about all this when it happened." J.D. walked up behind Sam. He'd left the clipboard on the podium desk and picked up a large padlock from a table nearby. "What do you think family's for, idiot?"

"Bustin' my chops, apparently." Luke fell into step as his brothers headed for the exit. "What about the theory that Barton Reid has formed his own private army?"

"Oh, I can tell you what's going on with that," J.D. said.

Both Sam and Luke stopped short, staring at their eldest brother. "Really?" Sam asked skeptically.

J.D. grimaced. "You two think you were the only guys who had to deal with State Department jerks like Reid? I spent six years in the Navy and six more in the Reserve. We ate State Department jerks for breakfast. If you want to know who's doing Reid's dirty work, look at an outfit called MacLear."

"The security company?" Luke asked. "It's one of the best in the business. Great reputation."

J.D. snorted. "For coverin' their tracks, maybe."

Luke glanced over at Sam. His brother shrugged.

"Jarheads," J.D. said with an exasperated growl, heading briskly out the door.

Sam and Luke scrambled after him, helping him close the heavy corrugated-metal doors. "What makes you connect MacLear to Barton Reid?" Luke asked.

J.D. padlocked the door, giving the lock a tug to make sure it was secure. "You know who Jackson Melville is, right?"

"MacLear's CEO," Sam answered.

"We served together on the same ship ten years ago. Total brownnoser and a real skate—never did anything he didn't have to. Lieutenant junior grade and going nowhere, career-wise. Drank too much, gambled too much and blamed all his mistakes on other crewmen." J.D. grimaced. "Then one day, the captain assigned Melville to babysit some State Department jerks. Barton Reid was one of 'em. Two weeks later, Melville was reassigned to the Pentagon permanently."

J.D. started walking toward the helicopter. Luke fell into step next to him, Sam on their heels. "And?"

"Suddenly he's getting promotions right and left, showing up on TV as a Pentagon spokesman and sometimes doing the Sunday morning shows," J.D. continued. "He retired to take over the helm of MacLear when Talmadge MacLear died three years ago."

Luke had to admit, the timing, along with the connection to Barton Reid, seemed pretty suspicious. MacLear had an excellent reputation in the business, but it wouldn't be the first time such a company turned out to have a seamy underbelly.

They reached the helicopter. Kristen and Abby were inside, settling Stevie into his car seat. Abby looked up and met Luke's gaze, a slight smile curving her lips. He smiled back, eager to tell her about J.D.'s theory. She was levelheaded; she'd tell him whether he was crazy to think his brother's conspiracy theory had some merit.

Kristen backed out of the helicopter and came to stand next to Sam. "You ready to hit the road?" she asked him.

Luke looked at his brother. "You're not flying with us?"

Sam shook his head. "I'm driving back with Kristen. Less weight in the bird will make the trip back safer and faster for you. We'll be back there sometime tomorrow. I'll find a way to see you and hopefully, I'll have more to tell you about both Reid and Cordero."

"Are you going to check into J.D.'s theory?"

"I'll ask around, see who knows what."

Luke reached out and gave his brother a fierce hug. "Thank you, man. I don't know what we'd have done without your help."

Sam pulled back, his expression serious. "Any new ideas about where Matt might have hidden whatever it was he took?"

"Oh, man—can't believe I forgot to tell you!" He told Sam his theory about the flash drives. "Last I heard, Hannah still had the one that wouldn't open."

Sam grinned. "I remember that! She was positive that whatever pictures were on the disk that wouldn't open had to be the best pictures ever, and she spent weeks fiddling with the file to figure a way past the password protection."

"Does she still have the flash drive?"

"Probably. She got sidetracked by the whole falling in love with a cowboy and getting married thing, and then having a baby. But you know her—I'd bet she's still got it. You can ask her when you touch down in Chickasaw County. She's supposed to be on the welcoming committee."

Luke gave Sam another hug. "See you soon. Thanks again."

Sam patted his shoulders. "You owe me, kid."

Luke knew his brother was right. He owed Sam more than he could ever hope to pay.

LUKE FELL ASLEEP almost as soon as the Bell 407 lifted off, the combination of sleepless nights and the relative security of being able to trust his safety to his brother's care allowing him to relax fully for the first time in days. Probably even years. He woke a couple of hours later as the helicopter began its descent to the Chickasaw County Aviation helipad.

Sam had been right. Luke's sister, Hannah, was waiting for their arrival, standing a safe distance from the helipad, next to a tall, rawboned man in a black Stetson who had to be her husband, Riley Patterson. Hannah waved excitedly as the helicopter touched down, and Luke grinned back at her.

God, he'd missed the little minx.

"That must be Riley," Abby murmured sleepily from beside him. "I hope he's heard from Jim and Rita and they're okay."

Luke caught her hand and gave it a quick squeeze. "Sam would have told me if they weren't."

"How far to the cabin?" She looked at Stevie, who was starting to fuss. The helicopter's engine had jarred him awake when they took off in Greenwood a couple of hours earlier. Abby had sat next to him for a while until he got used to the roar and settled back down to sleep. Now the silence of the shut-down engine had awakened him again.

Luke reached across and unbuckled Stevie from the safety seat. The little boy held out his arms eagerly, letting Luke pull him across the narrow space into his lap.

He cuddled his son close, smiling as Stevie curled up against him and patted his chest. He looked over at Abby and found her smiling at them, though a hint of regret darkened her blue eyes, giving his own happiness a bittersweet edge.

"The cabin's less than a mile from here. We'll be there in five minutes, unless they're sending us on mule or something."

Her eyes narrowed suspiciously. "Mule?"

He just grinned.

THE HELICOPTER'S rotor blades finally slowed to a stop, and Hannah and Riley moved forward to open the door. Hannah beamed up at Luke as he handed Stevie down to her waiting arms.

Stevie started protesting immediately. Luke hopped down and helped Abby out so she could take their squirming son from Hannah. Passing him over to Abby, Hannah quickly turned to Luke and threw herself into his arms.

The tight hug turned into a pummeling, as she rapped her small fists against his arms and back. "I can't believe you kept the Cordero stuff a secret from us this whole time! What were you thinking, you big idiot?"

Riley caught Hannah around the waist and pulled her off of Luke. "Settle down, Rocky Balboa." He reached his hand out to Luke. "I'm Riley. Nice to finally meet you."

Luke shook his brother-in-law's hand. "Same here. Thanks for the help in Yuma. Have you heard from your folks?"

"They're staying with Joe and Jane up in Canyon Creek for a while," Riley answered. "They'll be fine."

"If you talk to them, please be sure to tell them how sorry we are about what happened to their house," Abby interjected, bouncing Stevie on her hip. "I feel so horrible about that."

Hannah put her hand on Abby's shoulder. "Rita specifically said to tell you not to feel guilty. It was the most excitement they've had in years." Hannah smiled at her. "I'm Luke's sister, Hannah. I guess you figured that out, though."

Abby managed to smile, although Luke could tell she was practically dead on her feet. He needed to get them to the safety of the mountain cabin that his brothers and sister had set up for them to use.

Kristen had filled Abby in on the plan while Luke was in the hangar talking to J.D. and Sam about Barton Reid. The cabin was one of three larger properties that Cooper Cove Marina managed as a vacation rental. The three-bedroom log home was the most distant of the three from civilization but boasted all the modern amenities they'd need, including a wireless Internet connection and—as Abby had told him with obvious excitement—an enormous bathtub perfect for soaking in.

It was, by far, the most appealing fugitive hideout they could have hoped for.

Hannah turned to Luke with an apologetic expression. "I've got a six-o'clock appointment at the lake, so I have to run. Oh, but before I go—" Hannah reached into the pocket of her jeans and pulled out something about the size of a pack of gum. "Sam called and told me you might be needing this."

It was the flash drive.

"I can't promise it contains the files everybody's looking for, but it's the only one of the disks we couldn't open." Hannah handed it to him. He tucked it into the front pocket of his jeans, where it fit snugly enough to reassure him it wouldn't fall out on the ride to the cabin.

Hannah turned to look at Abby. "It's good to finally meet you, Abby. Luke used to write about you all the time in his letters home. I hope that disk is the answer to your problems."

Hannah gave Luke another hug, then kissed her husband and headed off, moving with more energy than anyone should be able to muster up at five-thirty on a cool November morning.

J.D. brought the last of their bags out of the helicopter and carried them over to Luke. "Y'all ready to head out?"

"Who's driving us?"

J.D. reached into his pocket and pulled out a set of keys. He tossed them to Luke. "I helped Cissy buy a new car for college, so y'all can take her old one." He motioned toward a blue Honda Civic parked nearby. He picked up a couple of their bags and started toward the Honda. Luke, Abby and Riley fell into step behind him, carrying the rest of their things.

Luke moved closer to Riley. "Hey, Riley—has anyone shown up, calling themselves Feds, looking for us?"

Riley shook his head. "No. Sam told us what happened in Texarkana, so we've been on the lookout. But nobody's come around. Weird, if you ask me. If I was a fake Fed, looking for y'all, this would be one of the first places I'd go."

Maybe Reid and his boys figured that with so many Coopers involved in law enforcement in Chickasaw County, playing Feds wouldn't be nearly as easy to get away with, Luke thought. But that wasn't necessarily good news. Without an official cover story to work with, Reid's enforcers would resort to stealth. And if they were as resourceful at stealth as they were at tracking, things were about to get a whole lot more dangerous.

THEY ARRIVED AT THE CABIN within minutes, and as the rental house came into full view, Abby saw that the word *cabin* was wholly inadequate. The log house was beautiful and enormous, with a wraparound porch on the bottom floor and a massive stone chimney. The morning sun, now creeping over the treetops to the east, bathed the reddish-brown logs with rosy light.

The door of the cabin opened and a man in his late twenties bounded out onto the porch, his face split by an enormous grin. He was tall, with short black hair and bright blue eyes that danced with delight at the sight of Luke.

Luke grinned back at him. "Good God, Aaron Cooper, just how tall did you grow, son?"

Aaron took the shallow porch steps in one leap and pulled his brother into a bear hug. "Six-five last I checked. God, it's great to see you."

Abby pulled Stevie from his safety seat and carried him to where Luke and Aaron stood grinning at each other. All the Cooper men she'd met were large, but Aaron topped them all by at least three inches, and he had the build of a football player.

"Aaron, this is Abby," Luke said. "Abby, my baby brother."

Aaron shook her hand, his gentle grip swallowing her hand whole. "And this is Stevie, I guess?"

Stevie looked up at Aaron from Abby's arms, his eyes wide. "Ooo," he crooned, apparently impressed by Aaron's sheer bulk.

"This is Stevie," Abby answered. "It's nice to meet you."

"Same here." Aaron looked over at his brother. "All the beds have clean sheets. The electricity and water have been turned on. Wi-Fi should work, too, if you need it. Everybody raided their own fridges and freezers so you'd have stuff to eat. Plus, I left a couple of rifles and an extra Smith & Wesson in the hall closet. The key's on a hook in the kitchen."

Abby hadn't used a gun since Stevie was born, but she'd been shooting rifles and pistols since she was a girl. She was a good markswoman, and if circumstances required her to use a weapon to protect her son, she was ready and willing to do it.

Luke retrieved their bags from the Honda's trunk. Aaron caught his arm. "Y'all have to be dog tired after all that running. Go inside. I'll be in with the bags in a minute."

"Aren't you on duty soon?" Luke asked. Aaron must be the brother who was a sheriff's deputy, Abby realized.

"I'm only on call on weekends now," Aaron answered, hauling all three bags out with deceptive ease.

"Whose backside did you kiss for duty hours like those?"

Aaron beamed at his brother. "I got a promotion. Just last week, matter of fact. You're looking at Chickasaw County's newest sheriff's department investigator."

"Congratulations!" Luke clapped his brother on the back.

"So I'm going to fill in down at the bait shop this morning," Aaron added, looking past Luke and Abby toward the cabin, a broad grin on his face.

Abby turned to see an older woman standing in the open doorway, her blue eyes bright with happy tears. Her gaze fixed on Luke, and Abby knew, without anyone telling her, that the woman was Luke's mother. There was no mistaking the joy of a mother seeing her child after a long absence.

Luke bounded up the porch steps and wrapped his arms around his mother. Abby felt tears pricking her own eyes at the sight.

Next to her, Aaron chuckled softly. "See? I always knew he was her favorite."

Abby dragged her gaze from the reunion and looked up at Aaron. "He's really missed you folks, you know."

"We missed him, too." Aaron reached out and ruffled Stevie's hair. "Hey, Stevie, you're in luck, dude. Your uncle Jake has a boy a couple years older than you are who just happens to be ready to pass along some of his old toys."

Abby flinched at Aaron's use of the word *uncle,* but if Aaron noticed, he didn't give any indication as he explained that Jake's stepson, Micah, had been happy to lose some of his old playthings once Jake offered to buy him some new toys as a reward for his generosity. "Greedy little devil went for that deal in a heartbeat," Aaron said with a fond grin.

Luke waved Abby up the stairs. "Mom, this is Abby Chandler and her son, Stevie. Abby, this is my mother, Beth Cooper."

Beth took Abby's free hand and gave it a motherly squeeze. "Sam told us what the three of you have been through over the past few days. I thought maybe you could use some uninterrupted sleep, so I'm here to watch after Stevie for you while the two of you have a rest."

The thought of a few hours of sleep in a real bed nearly brought tears to Abby's eyes. "Are you sure it's no trouble?"

"Positive." Beth smiled at Stevie. "In fact, I thought I could take him down to the house—Hannah has a fishing client this morning, so Riley's got Cody to himself for a few hours and offered to stick around the house with him so Stevie will have someone to play with."

"Having Riley there would be like having a bodyguard with him," Luke added softly. "Plus, Aaron will be right down the hill at the bait shop. And we're dead on our feet."

He was right. She and Luke were running on empty, while Stevie had managed to get several nights of sleep, despite their frantic flight eastward. Riley and Aaron were both sheriff's department deputies, and Stevie would be surrounded by people who'd gladly take a bullet for him, simply because Luke asked them to.

"Okay," she said.

"Why don't you take a bath?" Luke suggested, taking Stevie from her arms and handing him to Beth. "I know you want one."

More than words could say, she thought with a wry grin, pleased to see that Stevie was immediately taken with Luke's mother, who had come armed with a small toy truck which Stevie found instantly fascinating.

Luke led Abby inside the cabin, peeling her denim jacket off her arms and hanging it on the hand-carved coatrack by the door. Abby faltered to a stop a few feet inside the room, staring around in delight.

Kristen's description of the cabin hadn't come close to capturing the rustic charm of the place. The furnishings were an eclectic blend of handmade wood furniture and classic, sturdy manufactured pieces. The color scheme was mostly earth-toned neutrals, with splashes of color here and there, from a bright woven throw rug in front of the leather sofa to the rich autumn red of the canvas curtains on the windows.

"I'll play with Stevie in the playroom while the two of you get cleaned up," Beth suggested from behind them. "Come on, Stevie, let me show you your new toys!" She carried Stevie into a small sunroom just off the great room.

"Mother raised six boys," Luke said softly, as Abby's worried gaze followed her son and Beth into the other room. "I think she knows how to handle Stevie."

"He took right to her, didn't he?"

"Yeah." There was a bittersweet tone in Luke's voice, and Abby knew he was wishing it was safe to tell his mother that she had another grandson.

Unfortunately, they both knew that could never happen.

## Chapter Fifteen

The bathroom was everything Abby had hoped for, spacious and airy, with an enormous claw-foot tub that took up one end of the room. Next to it, the smaller shower cubicle seemed like an afterthought. Abby gave a soft murmur of delight.

"I figured you'd like it," Luke said with a smile. "I'm going to take a shower in the other bathroom. See you in a bit." He gave her shoulder a quick squeeze and was gone.

A comb, a brush and a small wicker basket containing bath gels, bath crystals, shampoos and lotions sat on a vanity table by the tub. Running hot water into the tub, Abby selected the nearest bottle of bubble bath and dumped in a generous amount. In seconds, apple-scented steam filled the room.

Easing into the hot water, she washed off what felt like days' worth of grime and settled back against the tub, letting herself relax for the first time since the moment she'd arrived home to find intruders in her house.

She might not be completely safe, but this was closer than she'd thought she'd ever be again.

Abby wasn't sure how long she'd been soaking when a soft knock on the door made her open her eyes. A second later, the door opened a few inches. "You haven't fallen asleep in there, have you?" Luke asked gently.

"Shh, you'll wake me," she answered just as quietly.

"Mom and Stevie are getting along like old pals, so she

took him on to the house. She's going to make pancakes for him and Cody." Luke slipped inside the bathroom, carrying a tray loaded with golden-brown muffins and steaming mugs of coffee. "She left us a little something for breakfast, as well."

Luke's shirt was unbuttoned, revealing the toned, battle-hardened body he'd earned in the Marines and apparently maintained even after his retirement. In comparison, she felt like a slob, with a small pregnancy pooch she hadn't yet been able to lose, and pale stretch marks that lined her sides. She sank lower under the bubbles, heat staining her cheeks, and tried to forget she was stark naked under the suds. "The muffins smell great."

Luke pulled the vanity bench next to the bath. "Mom's specialty. Banana nut muffins. Mmm." He pinched off a piece of muffin and held it in front of her mouth.

She opened her mouth and he placed the piece delicately on her tongue. Immediately, a rich, buttery sweet flavor filled her mouth, and she couldn't hold back a soft moan of delight.

"What did I tell you?" he murmured, pinching off another piece of muffin and popping it into his own mouth.

Languid heat flooded her body, threatening to destroy what was left of her self-control, but she clung to sanity. She and Luke couldn't be together, no matter how much either of them might want it. Stevie's safety had to come first. If Eladio Cordero found out that Luke had a son—

"Have you looked at the flash drive?" She shook her head when he offered another piece of muffin, no longer hungry.

Luke set the plate of muffins aside, his expression growing serious. "I took a quick look before I came in here. Definitely password-protected. Possibly encrypted as well, even though they're probably image files."

"How are you going to figure out the password?"

"It's got to be something Matt thought I'd figure out."

The water in the tub was turning cool, scattering goose bumps along her arms and legs. She pushed away the mild discomfort. "What about the encryption once we're into the file?"

"He wouldn't have had time to do anything fancy, so he probably went with the standard encryption we used for some of our more sensitive communications." Luke's gaze dropped from her face to her bare shoulders. "Is the water getting cold?"

She nodded. "I'm turning into a prune, anyway."

Luke pushed to his feet, though his gaze remained fixed on her bare skin for a moment. He took a deep breath and dragged his gaze away. "I'll wait outside."

"Actually, I left my clothes in the other room—"

"I'll get the bag for you." He headed out of the bathroom, closing the door behind him.

Abby pulled the drain on the tub and stepped out, dripping water and suds onto the fluffy bath mat protecting the floor by the tub. She hurried over to the detached shower and rinsed off the remaining suds, quickly giving her hair a quick lathering with the apple-scented shampoo sitting in the shower caddy.

By the time Luke knocked on the door again, she'd finished rinsing off and was wrapping herself in a large green bath towel. "Come in," she called.

Luke entered and stopped short, staring at her. "I—uh—here are your clothes." He handed her the bag, his fingers brushing against hers.

She swallowed a sudden lump in her throat. "Thanks." She took the bag and forced her feet into motion, heading for the door. She made it about two steps before Luke's hand closed around her arm, swinging her back around to face him.

The look in his eyes sent a shock wave through her entire

body. Fire burned there, along with a dark resolve that froze her breath in her lungs.

"You should walk out of here and not look back." Luke's voice moved through her like a tremor, setting her nerves to humming. "But you're not going to go, are you?"

Caught in the velvet snare of his hungry gaze, she couldn't have moved if she'd wanted to.

And she didn't want to.

"No," she admitted, giving up any pretense that she didn't want him every bit as much as he wanted her. It didn't matter that nothing good could come of what was about to happen between them. It didn't matter that loving him now would make it that much harder when she had to walk away again.

All that mattered was that they had been given one more chance to be with each other, with no lies or secrets between them, nothing to taint the connection that bound them together, for however short a time they might have.

Luke's fingers glided over her damp skin, up her arms to her shoulders. He lightly traced the ridges of her collarbones, his fingers meeting in the hollow of her throat and moving downward. They dipped into the cleft of her breasts, spreading heat through her flesh until she had to gasp for breath.

He pulled loose the tuck of the bath towel, which fell to the floor, leaving her bare beneath his hungry gaze.

She felt his scrutiny like a touch, moving over her, laying her bare, attributes and flaws alike. His fingers followed, skimming over the curve of her hips, up the faint furrows of stretch marks left by her pregnancy. He knelt on the floor in front of her, pressing his lips against the swell of her lower belly, where Stevie had grown and thrived for nine months.

He looked up at her, his eyes bright with emotion. "You're so beautiful." His voice was shaky and soft, sending a jolt of need racing through her to settle at her core.

Dropping to her own knees, she caught his face between

her hands, dragging her thumb across the softness of his lower lip. Unable to find words to answer him, she replied with a kiss, the only way she knew to impart to him the tangle of wild emotions filling her heart.

"Wait," he rasped, drawing away for a second. "I need to get something—"

She shook her head, reaching down to pick up the bag he'd dropped on the floor. She scrabbled through the side pocket and pulled out a small box of condoms. "Like this?"

He stared at the box, then back at her. "You, too? When?"

"Remember when we stopped for gas at that place back in Arkansas, and I went in to get some bottled water?" She grinned. "I figured it wouldn't hurt to be prepared, just in case."

The sizzling look he gave her sent another bolt of lightning shooting straight to her core. "In case you got the chance to seduce me?"

"In case you seduced me," she countered, sliding her hand down to the button of his jeans. "Because I knew I could never say no to you."

He stilled her fingers as she inched his zipper down. "Are you sure about this? You know there'll be no happy ending."

"I know," she said, closing her fingers around his and bringing them up to her lips. She kissed his knuckles lightly, one at a time, then squeezed his hands. "That's why I'm not going to turn down whatever you can offer. Even if this is all we ever get, it's still something. Isn't it?"

He cradled her face between his palms, gazing at her with such depth of emotion that she felt as if her bones had turned to liquid. "Yes," he answered, and lowered his head, his mouth slanting across hers in a deep, hungry kiss.

THE FISHING TRIP was going about the way Damon expected. He doubted that Tris and Malcolm were having any more luck fishing information out of Jake and Gabe Cooper than he was in getting Hannah Patterson to talk. Clearly, all the Coopers had circled the wagons to protect their brother. If he wanted to find out where Luke was now and if—or when—he'd be heading home to Gossamer Ridge, he'd probably have to find out from someone outside the family.

But who? He doubted any of the Coopers would let it slip, even to friends, if they'd heard anything from Luke. They all knew the danger in loose lips. So if anyone outside the family knew anything, it would be something learned by accident.

So think, Damon. Luke Cooper's coming home to Gossamer Ridge. He can't stay at a motel or anywhere he might come into contact with people who know him—there's an APB out on him and not even the Coopers can shove something like that in a drawer and forget it. So where would they stash him?

The fishing camp? He didn't know that much about places like fishing camps—was it basically a bunch of campsites? Were there cabins?

A tug on his fishing line distracted him for a moment. He reeled in a fat black crappie and grinned over at Hannah, playing the part of the carefree fisherman.

She smiled back at him. "That's a big one. You going to keep him? The limit's thirty, and that one's long enough—"

"I don't reckon my motel would appreciate me hauling in a mess of fish to store in the room fridge," Damon drawled, deliberately using the accent he'd left behind years ago.

"We can store it for you—just pick it up when you leave town. Or if you're thinking about extending the trip, you might consider staying at the fishing camp. We have a camp freezer where our guests can store their catches."

"What's the fishing camp like?" Damon asked, hardly able to believe that the distraction of catching the crappie had led him right into the topic he most wanted to discuss. "Do I need a tent or something?"

"We do have places for people to pitch tents, but we also have some cabins. There are several small ones closer to the water, or if you wanted something a little nicer and more secluded, we have a handful of larger cabins up the mountainside." She clamped her mouth shut suddenly. "Actually, I think all of those are booked this week, but the smaller cabins are very nice, and since you're here to fish anyway—"

*Bingo,* Damon thought, not missing the sudden flush darkening her face. She'd been too quick to tell him that the mountain cabins were already occupied.

Occupied by her brother and Abby Chandler, perhaps?

A vibration against his left hip interrupted his thoughts. He quickly unhooked the fish and considered whether or not it would look more authentic to keep the crappie or toss it back in the lake. He opted for the latter—no reason to kill the fish since he didn't intend to hang here long once he found what he was looking for.

"Maybe next trip," he said, pulling the cell phone from his pocket. "I've got to check this—might be from the office."

Hannah nodded and turned her attention back to the trolling motor, moving them a little farther out into the lake.

There was a text message waiting. Damon opened it. It was from Tris.

CHANDLER BOY HERE @ BAIT SHOP. WILL SCOOP & GRAB ASAP.

Damon struggled to keep his outward demeanor calm, but inside, he'd gone utterly cold. He'd been so sure he was about to find Cooper and the Chandler woman, and now everything was about to go to hell.

He had to get to the bait shop first. The last thing he could afford to do was let Tris and Malcolm get to the kid first and use him to extract the missing files from his mother and Cooper. It would ruin all his plans.

But what if he was already too late?

ABBY GAZED UP at the ceiling, where morning sunlight filtering through the curtains painted undulating bands of light across the white expanse. Her body felt heavy and completely sated, so utterly content that she decided she didn't want to move for the rest of the day.

Luke traced the swell of her breast, sending little sparks fluttering through her, but she felt too weak to be roused to anything more strenuous than a lazy smile. "Are you going to just lie there all day?" he murmured, nuzzling her shoulder.

"Is that a problem?"

He lowered his mouth to her breast, covering one nipple and suckling lightly. Her sex contracted, suggesting she wasn't entirely spent.

He lifted his head, resting his chin on her sternum. "I wish we had days to do nothing more than this."

A sliver of darkness invaded the warm cocoon of contentment their passion had wrapped around them. "But we don't have days, do we?" she sighed, stroking his hair.

"The sooner we figure out the password to the flash drive, the sooner we can stop the people who are threatening you and Stevie." Luke caught her hand, kissing her fingertips. "You want that, don't you?"

Of course she wanted Stevie to be safe. She wanted to be able to go anywhere she wanted and not worry that someone was coming after her. The contents of that flash drive might give them the ammunition to take down Barton Reid and his private army.

But it would also put an end to any reason Luke had to stay around her and Stevie anymore. He could walk away, sparing them from the deadly attention of Eladio Cordero and *Los Tiburones*.

"Does it have to be over?" she asked quietly.

He knew what she was asking. "You know it does."

Did she? Or did Cordero already suspect, thanks to Luke's decision to help her with Reid's thugs, that she and Stevie were important to Luke? Important enough to use to punish him?

Before she could voice her thoughts, Luke rolled away from her and sat up on the edge of the bed. "I'm going to go take a shower and see what I can rustle up for lunch." He shot her a wicked look. "Want to join me?"

She wanted to say no, to make him stop and talk to her about the future. But she knew his mind was made up. Whatever happened here, in this temporary sanctuary, might be all they'd ever have together.

She managed to smile, though a dull ache had set up residence in the center of her chest. "Race you there!"

AN HOUR LATER, they made it to the kitchen. While Abby contemplated how to bring up the subject of their future again, Luke raided the refrigerator for bread, sandwich meat, mayonnaise and mustard. "What're you in the mood for? Ham?"

She caught his hand, removing the butter knife and laying it on the counter. "I'm in the mood to talk about what happens when this mess with the flash drive is over."

A pained look flashed in his eyes. "You know what happens. Y'all go back to San Diego. Or Texas—you were happy in Texas. Billy and Wanda would love to have you there fulltime."

"Ross, too, I guess," Abby said.

Luke flinched visibly.

"But I don't want to be with Ross. I want to be with you."

He clasped her hands in his, pulling her closer. "I want to be with you, too. But you know it can't happen."

"What if it can?" She slid closer, flattening her breasts against his chest. "We can find a way to make it work—"

He caught her arms and gently pushed her away. "How about we concentrate on finding out what's on that disk?" He edged past her, ignoring the food he'd laid out, and headed into the great room, where his laptop computer was already set up, with the flash drive in place.

Disheartened by his refusal to consider other options, she put the food back in the refrigerator and joined him on the sofa. "You have a bad habit of having your way with me, then walking away," she muttered.

He looked at her, his mouth trembling open as if he wanted to respond, but he clamped his lips shut and turned back to the computer. He typed the word *Tesoro* in the prompt box. A response flashed up on the screen. "Incorrect Password."

"Try the date Matt and I married—June 11," Abby suggested.

Luke typed in several variations of the date, including the year, excluding the year, excluding the day. Nothing worked.

"I tried our birthdays earlier, with no luck," he told her.

"How about *Janis Meeks?*" she murmured, surprised that she didn't even feel a twinge of hurt anymore at the thought of Matt's infidelities. Maybe the pain of knowing she'd have to walk away from Luke all too soon was enough to eclipse the humiliation of her husband's lies.

Luke typed the name in as one word, no spaces. A few seconds passed without anything happening.

Then a folder flashed onto the screen, filled with a series of image files.

"They're encrypted," Luke said a few minutes later, "but I'm pretty sure I know the program he used." He opened a program and started dragging the files into the decryption queue. Slowly, thumbnail images began to pop into a second box. When the program finished, Luke opened the first file.

It was a scan of a ledger. Abby read over the notations, trying to make sense of what they revealed. "It's a record of payments," she said, "but what do those letters mean?" She pointed to a series of capital letters listed by each number.

"Those are acronyms for the weapons they were providing to *El Cambio*," Luke answered. "Grenade launchers, anti-aircraft missiles, all kinds of service rifles—" He frowned darkly. "Son of a bitch!"

"I thought they were trading arms for drugs, not money."

Luke looked at the next few files. "They were. The money seems to denote the street value of the drugs they were handing over to Voices for Villages in exchange for the guns."

"Why would they keep such detailed records of illegal activities?"

"So nobody got cheated. They had to be able to produce proof that the deals were equitable or *El Cambio* might have used force to get what they wanted." Luke sighed. "I think Matt got these files from Janis Meeks somehow."

"I bet that's where he was going all those nights—" Abby sighed. "Before his last tour of duty, he'd always left his overseas dalliances behind when he came home. At least, before then, I'd never had any reason to doubt he was staying faithful to me while he was home."

"He was seeing Janis Meeks stateside?" Luke frowned.

"He was seeing someone," she answered. "Going out at all hours, not telling me anything about what he was doing—his behavior during those last weeks at home was what eventually led me to find out about all the other times he'd cheated." She'd asked a lot of questions after his death. She hadn't liked many of the answers she'd found.

They pored through the rest of the files, which were far more thorough than even Luke had seemed to expect. There were names, dates, exchanges that would be easy for prosecutors to verify, even if the original files had been destroyed. There were also copies of e-mails from Barton Reid, establishing his direct knowledge of the illegal arms-for-drugs trade.

"This will bring down Reid for sure," Luke said as he copied the information onto his hard drive before removing the flash drive. "We just have to figure out which government agency we can trust not to sweep the information under the rug."

"We should make another copy. Just in case."

"I'll let you do that," he said, motioning for her to come with him. Abby followed him to the hall closet, which he had apparently already unlocked, since he opened it without a key. Inside, she saw a couple of rifles with several ammunition magazines stacked nearby, and a gun box which must contain the Smith & Wesson Aaron had mentioned.

Luke pulled a small key ring from his pocket and opened the gun box, extracting a Smith & Wesson M&P Compact 9mm pistol. He checked the clip. Abby saw it was full.

He handed her the pistol. He knew she knew how to use one.

She took it from him, let herself get used to the weight and the shape. Luke and Matt had both taken her to the firing range now and then, so she could stay in practice. She hadn't been back since Matt's death, but she thought she'd be able to hold her own if the worst happened.

Now that they'd found the flash drive, maybe the worst wouldn't have to happen at all—

The phone in the great room rang, making Abby jump.

"Nobody would be calling here except family," Luke murmured, moving past her into the great room. He picked up the phone. "Yeah?"

As Abby joined him at the table, his forehead creased in a deep frown. He looked down at her, his expression odd.

"Who is it?" Abby whispered.

"It's Hannah," he answered, confusion wrinkling his brow. "She says her fishing client insists on speaking to you."

# Chapter Sixteen

Abby stared at Luke, confused. "What?"

"Hannah said it was important. I trust her. I think you'd better talk to the man." Luke handed her the phone.

Abby's hand shook so much she almost dropped the phone. "This is Abby Chandler."

The voice that greeted her was male, deep and familiar. It was the second man from her apartment, she realized immediately. "Mrs. Chandler, my name is Damon Sanford. I'm connected with the people who are after you, but I am not on their side. I met you before at your apartment."

"I remember."

"It's very important that you believe what I'm saying to you. I know you have every reason to doubt me, so I'm going to give you a name. Alexander Quinn. I want you to ask Luke Cooper if he's ever heard of the man. Ask him now."

She looked at Luke. "Do you know an Alexander Quinn?"

Luke blinked with surprise. "CIA handler. Worked in the American embassy in Sanselmo when I was there three years ago."

"He says Quinn is a CIA agent," Abby said into the phone.

"Quinn will be calling him in five minutes. He needs to listen to what Quinn tells him to do. We may already be too late to stop the abduction of your son, so it's vital that we have a plan to get him back. Understand?"

Knees buckling, she fell to the sofa. "They have my son?"

"They sent me a text message, telling me they'd spotted him. I believe they were on their way to take him, and now Hannah Patterson can't get anyone to answer at the bait shop."

Luke's cell phone rang, making Abby's nerves jangle. He took it, stepping away from her for a moment.

"What's going on?" Damon asked.

"Luke just got a call." The thundercloud expression on Luke's face made her fear the worst.

"On my way," he said into the phone, then rang off. He turned to Abby, his voice hard. "Who are you talking to?"

"One of the men who've been following us. He says his name is Damon."

Luke grabbed the phone from Abby's nerveless fingers. "Hello, Damon. This is Luke Cooper. The sons of bitches you work with have taken Stevie." His voice grew cold and hard. "I hope you weren't attached to them."

Abby's heart stuttered. "They have Stevie?"

Luke hung up and grabbed his jacket. "Riley and Aaron have both been shot. Dad got there just after the ambush."

"Are they—?"

"They're alive. Ambulances are on the way."

"What about your mother?"

"Shaken up and mad as hell. Once they took out Aaron and Riley, they knocked her around and grabbed Stevie."

"Luke, no—" She stared at him, her heart stuttering.

"I've got to go." He crossed to the table and took the flash drive out of the laptop's USB port. "If this is what it takes to get Stevie back, then it's what it takes."

She rose to her feet, nervous energy overcoming her earlier shock. "They've got to know you'd make a copy."

"Lock the laptop in the closet and take out whatever you need to hold off intruders. I'll call as soon as I know anything." He closed his hand over the back of her neck and pulled her to him, covering her mouth with a hard, fierce kiss. "Stay alive," he murmured, then let her go. "I'll call soon."

He left the cabin, not looking back.

THE SCENE AT the bait shop was pure chaos. Fire trucks, police cruisers and a couple of ambulances filled the parking lot, and the whole area crawled with men and women in uniform. Luke spotted Aaron sitting on a gurney in front of one of the ambulances, his left upper arm wrapped in a large white bandage. He was arguing with the emergency medical technician trying to coax him into the ambulance.

"I'm not going to the damned hospital," Aaron growled, pushing to his feet. He spotted Luke and moved the EMT aside, crossing quickly to his brother's side. "Sons of bitches shot me from behind, shoved me into the bait room and locked me in."

"Where's Riley?"

Aaron nodded toward the second ambulance, where Riley Patterson was giving his own technician a hard time, trying to rise from the gurney where he sat. "Grazed his skull and knocked him out. Then the bastards got to Mom and grabbed the kid."

Luke tried not to picture how the snatch-and-grab must have gone down. He prayed the men wouldn't hurt Stevie before he found them. "Mom's okay?"

"She'll be fine. She's just furious." Aaron examined the bandage on his arm. "I'm sorry, man. You trusted us to take care of the kid—"

"You can't stop bullets," Luke said firmly. What had

happened to Stevie was his own fault. He should never have allowed the boy out of his sight for a second.

"The guys who shot me—they were Gabe's fishing clients this morning. Nobody's seen or heard from Gabe." Aaron's voice went raspy a second. "I'm going to kill those sons of bitches."

"Not if I get there first."

"Mom says they headed into the woods on foot. They know you're here somewhere. Maybe they guessed you'd be stashed in one of the cabins."

*Abby,* Luke thought, his stomach knotting. She'd be a sitting duck. "Are you okay, Aaron? Good enough to back me up if I need it?"

Aaron nodded. "One good arm left. I can still shoot."

Luke laid his hand on his brother's face, tamping down the emotion that threatened to paralyze him. "See if you can get J.D. on the phone. I need Sam and Kristen here, even if he has to go get them in that helicopter and bring them back."

"Sam called in just before this all happened. He's an hour away, tops. They made good time on the trip back."

"Stay in touch with him. Get us plenty of backup from the sheriff's department and the Gossamer Ridge police, too." He dropped his hand and headed over to the other ambulance to check on his brother-in-law.

Riley had talked his way off the gurney. "I'm fine."

"You were out at least a minute. You said so yourself," the female EMT said flatly. "You probably have a concussion."

"Not the first, won't be the last." Spotting Luke, Riley sidestepped the technician. "Have you heard from Hannah?"

"Talked to her a few minutes ago. She was fine." At least, he hoped she was. She and that Damon character should have gotten here by now.

The sound of a boat motor rose above the chaos surrounding him. Riley peered over the gathered crowd. "That's her boat."

Luke followed his brother-in-law's gaze and saw Hannah's boat pull up to the dock. A tall, well-built black man was in the boat with her. So was a soaking-wet Gabe Cooper.

"Thank God," Luke murmured, hurrying to the dock. Riley and Aaron were right behind him, there to help the man named Damon help Gabe out of the boat.

"Riley!" Hannah's face went pale at the sight of the bloody bandage on the side of her husband's head.

Riley pulled her into a fierce hug. "You've been telling me to get a haircut—"

"Not funny!" Hannah looked at Luke. "We found Gabe in the water—the bastards coldcocked him and threw him in the lake."

"I woke up fast when I hit the water." Gabe's teeth chattered wildly. "Thought I'd freeze to death before I got to shore, though. Thank God Hannah spotted me."

"Get him up to the house and into warm clothes," Luke said. "I need him battle-ready as soon as possible."

"Where's Cody?" Hannah asked, panic rising in her voice.

"He's okay—they didn't touch him." Riley cradled Hannah's face in his palms. "Everybody's okay."

She reached up to touch the bandage on her husband's head. "*You're* not okay."

"I'm fine."

"So'm I, thanks for askin'," Aaron drawled.

Hannah dragged her eyes away from Riley. "They shot you, too?" She looked up at Luke. "Who *are* these people?"

"They're employees of MacLear Enterprises," Damon said, impatience infusing his deep voice. "From a section called Special Services Unit. The two who attacked your family are named Tristan Hennessey and Malcolm Holly. Not their real names."

"Is Damon your real name?" Luke asked, equally impatient.

"No. I'm undercover at MacLear. I actually work for a company called Chimera Security."

"Never heard of it."

"Not under that name, no." Damon's teeth flashed in a grim smile. "My division does things that the government can't—or won't—do. Such as infiltrate a private firm like MacLear."

"Why?" Luke countered.

"To find out who's financing MacLear's special projects."

"Barton Reid," Luke said impatiently.

That seemed to surprise the man. "How do you know that?"

Luke ignored the question. "Where are Hennessey and Holly?"

"I got a text from them a couple of minutes ago. They've tracked down the record of the helicopter trip that brought you here last night. They're sure you're holed up in one of the Cooper Cove guest cabins."

Abby. They were going after Abby.

Luke took off at a run, trying frantically to remember the cabin number as he pulled out his phone. He had to warn Abby.

"Wait!" Damon raced after him, catching up at a dead sprint. He grabbed Luke's arm, whirling him around.

"Back off!" Luke growled, jerking his arm away.

"They're not alone," Damon warned him. "MacLear is sending backup. They'll be here within the hour."

Luke dropped the phone to his side. "How many?"

"Six, including me. But they have an office in Atlanta and

access to private helicopters and jets—they can have a dozen more here within an hour or two."

Hannah, Riley, Gabe and Aaron caught up with them in time to hear Damon's warning.

"We can have the sheriff's department SWAT team here in ten minutes," Aaron said.

"We may not have ten minutes," Luke warned. "I'm heading to the cabin to see if I can waylay Hennessey and Holly."

"I'll go with you," Gabe said through chattering teeth.

"You're going to the house to change into dry clothes," Luke said firmly. "Drink something hot. We'll need you before this is over, believe me."

"I'll go with you," Riley said.

"Nobody goes with me. The more people running around in the woods, the easier they'll spot us. I need the rest of y'all to gather up all the reinforcements you can get. Make sure Sam and Kristen get here as fast as possible, even if you have to send J.D. after them in that damned helicopter. Get all the firepower and ammunition you can find. We might need it. Damon can fill y'all in on what to expect." He turned urgently to Hannah. "What's the number of that damned cabin?"

DON'T THINK ABOUT STEVIE.

Abby zipped her olive drab jacket, glad she'd packed it back in San Diego four days ago. Was it really just four days? San Diego seemed like another lifetime.

For the fourth time since Luke had left the cabin, she checked the clip of the Smith & Wesson, reassuring herself that it was fully loaded. The gun box had contained an extra magazine, which she filled with more ammunition and stashed in her jacket pocket. Each clip held twelve rounds, plus there was a round already chambered in the pistol. She'd have twenty-five shots if she needed them.

She prayed she wouldn't need them.

*They won't hurt Stevie. Not yet. He's leverage.*

Luke had told her to stay here. Protect the laptop. But if he thought she was going to sit around in this cabin while her son was out there—

*They won't mistreat him. They need him to cooperate.*

She'd protect the laptop, she thought, reaching back to check for the small bundle duct-taped to her back, beneath three layers of clothing. She'd just protect it her own way. She'd also copied the files Luke had stored on the laptop onto a flash drive she'd found in the bottom of her purse.

The cabin phone rang, the sound harsh and jarring. Abby pressed her lips to a tight line to keep them from trembling and grabbed the phone. "Hello?"

"Abby, there are two men heading your way. Tristan Hennessey and Malcolm Holly. You've met Tristan. I don't know if they have figured out which cabin you're in yet, but they'll be coming. I need you to get out of the cabin and find somewhere to hunker down in the woods. Don't worry about the laptop or anything else. Just get yourself out of there and get hidden in the woods. You think you can do that?"

Abby smiled grimly. "I can."

"He's going to be okay, Abs. They have every reason to take good care of Stevie—"

"He's leverage," she finished for him.

"Go. I'll find you." He rang off.

Abby hung up and picked up the backpack she'd filled a few minutes ago. She'd found the lightweight pack in the bottom of Luke's duffel bag, already outfitted with survival basics like a flashlight, waterproofed matches, a water canteen and several protein bars. She'd added more supplies of her own, including a soft-sided first-aid kit and some juice boxes she'd found in the refrigerator. Stevie was small and might dehydrate sooner than an adult would. She had to be prepared in case they had to hide out in the woods longer than expected.

*Stevie's going to be all right. Because I'm going to get him back.*

She strapped the pack to her back and walked to the nearest window, peering through a narrow gap in the curtains. She stayed very still, letting her eyes adjust to the bright sunlight outside. The glare off the windows would provide limited protection from watching eyes, but any movement would give away her position.

A light breeze blew through the woods outside, the rustle of dying fall leaves audible even within the cabin. Abby scanned the woods, a section at a time, just as her father had shown her all those years ago when he taught her how to hunt. She'd been too tenderhearted to be any good at the sport, but she'd enjoyed the one-on-one time with her father, and he'd turned her into a pretty decent woodsman.

She was losing precious time, looking for possible intruders, but she saw it as a calculated trade-off. Luke wanted her to get to safety. She wanted something different.

She wanted to get her son back. Now.

There. Movement south of the cabin. She waited out the seconds that passed before she spotted movement again in the same area. A sandy-haired man dressed in a dark green jacket moved in a slow, stealthy zigzag toward the cabin, taking advantage of the cover provided by tree trunks and underbrush. The path he traveled followed a gentle incline upward, giving her the advantage of high ground. He was more exposed in the woods than she was in the house.

Of course, that could change at any moment.

She moved back slowly from the window and headed toward the back of the cabin, where a mudroom led out to a small stone patio about sixty yards from a bluff overlooking the lake. She had less room to maneuver out back, the drop-off limiting her means of escape. Of course, the intruders faced a similar downside. There was nowhere to hide behind the cabin.

The house phone rang, making her jump. Luke again? It had to be, didn't it?

What if something had happened to Stevie?

She returned to the great room and picked up the phone, her heart pounding. "Hello?"

She recognized the man's Boston accent immediately. "Hello, Mrs. Chandler. Nice to talk to you again."

"I want my son back."

"I want what your husband took."

"You don't even know what my husband took, Tristan," she answered coldly, anger giving her courage.

Her use of his name shocked him into silence for a moment.

She followed her advantage. "My husband stole files. Photocopies of ledgers proving that Voices for Villages facilitated the illegal trade of arms for drugs. They document e-mail correspondence between Voices for Villages director Janis Meeks and State Department South American liaison Barton Reid that show Reid's direct knowledge of the illegal arms trade and subsequent facilitation of further transactions."

"Indeed," he said calmly, although she heard an undertone of consternation. "Congratulations for finding the information. Now you have something to trade for your son's life."

Abby managed a grim smile, the weight of the laptop's hard drive heavy where it was strapped to her back. "Where are you? I'll bring it to you now."

She heard a soft grunting noise on the other end of the line, then silence.

"Hello?" she said into the phone.

The call disconnected.

Her heart in her throat, she ran to the window and looked outside. She didn't wait long to spot movement this time.

The woods were crawling with men.

She counted ten at first flush, all raven-haired and swarthy-skinned. They were dressed in woodland fatigues, armed to the teeth. A few wielded small machetes, hacking through the underbrush as they moved relentlessly toward the cabin.

Abby's blood turned to ice.

*Los Tiburones.*

She had run out of time and options. The back exit was her only choice. She ran to the back of the house and took a quick look out the window to make sure none of the men had circled around the back yet. The backyard was clear.

She pulled the Smith & Wesson 9mm from the side holster tucked into the waistband of her jeans, then headed out the back door as quietly as she could. She was left with only one route of escape now. The bluff.

She stayed low and went straight toward the drop-off, using the house as cover between herself and the approaching men. At the edge, she saw that the drop wasn't as precipitous as she'd feared. It was steep, but not impassable if she took care.

But before she could make another move, she heard a sound that froze her firmly in place.

"Mama!" It was Stevie's voice.

And he was close.

A TWIG SNAPPED behind him.

Sheltered by the low-hanging branches of a young pine, Luke scanned the woods for movement. He was a quarter mile from the cabin now, approaching from the bluff side, which added precious minutes to his mission. But this angle of attack would also give him the advantage of surprise.

"Caught me." The voice, coming from impossibly nearby, belonged to the man who called himself Damon. He stepped into the open from behind a nearby oak, hands raised in surrender.

"I should shoot you right now," Luke growled.

"Got a text message. My team was ambushed. Malcolm is wounded. He thinks Tris is dead."

"What about Stevie?" Luke asked urgently.

"He got away. Malcolm couldn't follow—his leg is broken."

Luke went cold, his mind searching for a scenario that didn't end in disaster. "Who ambushed them?"

Damon didn't have to answer. The truth burned in his eyes.

"Oh, God." *Los Tiburones.*

"Malcolm says there are a dozen of them, armed with rifles and machetes. They used a machete on Tris." Damon looked grim.

"Where's Malcolm now?"

"About fifty yards from the cabin, holed up behind a bush."

Fifty yards from the cabin. Was Stevie old enough to know to look for shelter?

Suddenly, he heard a cry. Distant but audible. "Mama!"

His heart in his throat, he began running uphill toward the sound. He heard Damon behind him, keeping pace. The cabin came into view over the bluff, then Luke was at the edge. He peered over, spotting a flash of dark green disappearing around the side of the cabin. Abby? If she'd been hiding out here, waiting for him, and heard her son's cry—

A gunshot rang out. *"¡Alto!"* a man's voice called out.

Luke held his breath.

Then he heard Abby's voice, loud and clear. "Who are you? What do you want?"

For a second, all he felt was sheer relief. She was still

alive. Then the truth hit him like a two-ton truck. His worst nightmare had come true.

*Los Tiburones* had the woman he loved. And it was only a matter of time before they killed her.

## Chapter Seventeen

Luke hauled himself over the edge of the bluff and raced to the back door of the cabin, praying Abby hadn't thought to lock it. It opened easily and he slipped inside, listening for movement within.

There was nothing.

Both rifles were still in the closet, as was his laptop, which lay on the floor. He grabbed a rifle and two of the ammunition magazines.

Hearing the back door open, he wheeled around, leveling the rifle at the intruder.

It was Damon, who raised his hands quickly. "Don't shoot."

Luke lowered the weapon to his side slowly.

Damon eyed the rifle. "Got another one of those?"

Luke weighed his distrust of the man against the odds stacked against them and pulled the spare rifle from the closet. He handed it to Damon, along with another magazine and a box of rounds.

Damon started loading it. "They've got the woman. I didn't see the kid."

Luke hurried to the front window, peering through the narrow gap in the curtains, which gave him a decent view of the woods just to the south of the cabin. It didn't take long to spot a clump of men gathered in a tight huddle. They weren't exactly hiding.

One of them moved, and Luke caught sight of Abby standing in the center, her hands held behind her back by one of the men.

Luke's heart contracted into a painful knot. She was still alive. She looked scared but unhurt. Damon was right. No sign of Stevie.

"How'd they know to come here?" he murmured aloud. "Last we knew, they were wreaking havoc in Arizona."

Damon didn't answer.

Luke turned to look at him. "Reid tipped them off?"

"I think so," Damon admitted.

"Just to take me out of the equation?"

"Probably thinks she'd be easier to manipulate alone."

"*Los Tiburones* aren't after me, Damon."

Damon looked confused. "They're not?"

"They want to force me to watch them torture and kill people I love." Like Abby and Stevie.

Damon looked sick. "God."

Luke strapped the rifle over his shoulder. "Stay here. Don't shoot unless it's to protect yourself or Abby."

"You're going after the kid?"

Luke slipped out the back without answering. Scanning the area, he still heard the murmur of voices from the woods in front of the cabin. He heard Abby's voice again, though he couldn't make out her words.

The voices were coming from the east. He thought back to the moment he'd heard the cry in the woods. It had come from the west, hadn't it? In the woods on the opposite side of the cabin from where *Los Tiburones* congregated now.

*Los Tiburones* weren't a conventional army. They were criminals Eladio Cordero had pulled from the streets of Tesoro to build his own crew of enforcers. What little they knew about covert ops they'd learned in the Sanselmo jungle, evading capture by the hapless *Guardia Nacional*.

Now that they had Abby, they would stay put, trying to figure out how to use her to flush out Luke.

He headed west, close to the bluff, keeping the cabin between him and *Los Tiburones* until the trees thickened a few yards down the bluff. Then he slipped into the woods and began looking for Stevie.

Fifty yards in, the metallic stench of blood assailed his nostrils. He followed the scent trail to a thicket of wild mountain laurel, where labored breathing gave away the position of the man Damon had called Malcolm.

He was too far gone to even lift his weapon when he saw Luke. Jerking the .357 Magnum from Malcolm's hand, Luke tucked the revolver into his jacket pocket and checked the man's injuries. The left leg of his jeans was soaked with blood, his belt acting as a makeshift tourniquet. But blood still oozed from the deep cut in the man's calf.

"Where's Stevie?"

"Tris screamed. Didn't…want…the kid…in the middle…." Malcolm's eyes fluttered shut.

Luke checked his pulse. Still there, slow and weak. He ripped open the man's bloody trousers and saw that the machete had cut to the bone, slicing through God knew how many vital blood vessels.

Luke dialed the number of the cabin. After several rings, Damon answered, his voice wary.

"I've found Malcolm," Luke said tersely. He described where he was. "I need you to call in his position to the bait shop so the EMTs will know where to look when they're allowed to come up here." Luke hung up without waiting for Damon's reply.

Tightening the tourniquet to stanch the oozing blood flow from Malcolm's leg, he wiped his bloody hands on the man's jacket and headed deeper into the woods, hoping Stevie had run away from the noise instead of toward it.

Within thirty yards, he heard snuffling sounds, faint but unmistakable. "Stevie," he breathed, trying to orient himself toward the sound. A little hiccuping noise, louder than the snuffles, came from his right. His heart hammering with relief, he spotted his son's blue jacket behind the trunk of a hickory tree ten feet away.

The little boy looked up at his approach, his tear-reddened eyes brightening at the sight of Luke. "Home!" he demanded, raising his arms.

Luke scooped Stevie up and hugged him tightly, his heart so full of love he thought it would explode. "Oh, baby, you're okay, aren't you?"

He looked the child over for injuries. Stevie's hands were scratched, probably from stumbling through the tangle of underbrush, and he was a filthy mess. But otherwise, he looked fine.

Luke kissed his grimy forehead. "Got to get you to safety so I can help your mama."

"Mama?" Stevie echoed, looking around expectantly.

"Mama's going to be fine," Luke vowed. But first, he had to get Stevie to safety.

He moved steadily westward, until he felt he was safe to stop and make another call.

Aaron answered on the first ring. "Luke?"

"I'm in the woods just west of the cabin. There are a dozen men in the woods east of the cabin. They have Abby. I have Stevie." He looked at his son. "Time to call in the cavalry."

THE MEN DIDN'T KNOW what to do with her, Abby realized. Much like the two men who'd broken into her apartment, Eladio Cordero's thugs seemed to function as pawns in a bigger game, moving various pieces around the board without any way of scoring the final coup.

Only four of the men surrounding her had spoken. One of them, Ramon, seemed to be the leader of the pack. Though he spoke a slang-filled version of Spanish typical of the southern slums of Sanselmo's capital, he was the one calling the shots. Still, Abby had the feeling he was waiting for further orders from someone higher up.

Cordero himself?

He'd want to savor Luke's suffering personally rather than hear about it at second hand. Was that why the men hadn't killed her already? Were they waiting for Cordero himself to arrive?

Suddenly, Ramon grabbed her arm roughly. *"¡Vamonos!"*

Abby pretended she didn't comprehend, not wanting her captors to know she could understand their every word. "What are you doing? Where are you taking me?"

Ramon just pulled her with him toward the cabin. Abby hid her panic. If they holed up inside, the situation could easily devolve into a hostage standoff.

Although inside, there were a couple of rifles that only she and Luke knew about....

She pretended to stumble, crying out loudly in feigned pain. If Luke was anywhere in the area, he'd be alerted.

God knew, she could use a diversion anytime now.

LUKE FROZE IN THE cabin's back doorway. Had that been a woman's scream?

Damon met him in the kitchen doorway. His expression softened with relief when he spotted Stevie, but hardened again. "They're bringing her this way. I think they're going to come inside."

Luke tucked Stevie closer. "Damn it. I'm not ready."

"I got a message from the MacLear backup team, too. They're in Gossamer Ridge, staging down near the lake."

"You still have the number to the marina? Call Hannah. Tell her to divert Riley and the local cops to their coordinates. Tell them your buddies are armed and dangerous." While Damon stepped away to make the call, Luke looked down at Stevie, his mind racing.

The safest place for the boy would be the attic. Any flying bullets would have to go two floors to reach him. Luke ran for the stairs, taking them two at a time.

The attic was little more than an inverted V-shaped crawl space between the ceiling of the second story and the gabled roof, but Stevie would be as safe here as anywhere.

"Do you know how to play hide-and-seek, Stevie?"

Stevie's eyes lit up. "Hide!"

"I want you to hide here, Stevie. Stay right behind this box, you see?" He lowered Stevie to the floor and showed him where to hide. "I'm going to find your mama and we'll surprise her, okay? Hide here and be very quiet."

Stevie squatted behind the box, grinning at Luke. He put one finger across his mouth. "Shh!"

Luke's insides melted at the sight of his son's delight, but he fought the emotion. There was no time. He locked the attic door, knowing he could pick it open later, and ran down the stairs.

At the second-floor landing, he heard footsteps racing up toward him. Damon came into view. "They're coming in."

Luke glanced at his watch. Some of his brothers might be in position by now.

He flipped open his phone. Nothing happened. Dead battery. Luke hissed a string of profanities.

"Use mine." Damon handed over the phone.

All the numbers were saved into his phone—he'd pro-

grammed them in before heading back into the woods earlier.
He didn't remember any of them.

Sam. He knew Sam's disposable phone number by heart.

He punched in the number. Sam answered on the first ring,
his voice wary. "Sam's Pizza."

"It's me. I'm on a borrowed phone. Where are you?"

"Sixty yards from the cabin. Made it home in time to get
in on the action."

Luke felt a flood of relief. He hadn't realized how much
he'd needed Sam to be there. "I'm inside. *Los Tiburones* are
here. They have Abby."

"I know. They left seven men outside. There are seven of
us. Want us to get the party started?"

*Los Tiburones* had left Abby alive this long for a reason.
Would they protect her, as he'd done with Stevie, at the first
sound of gunfire outside?

He looked at Damon. "You set to fight for the good guys
this time?"

Damon gave a nod.

"Go for it, Sam." He looked at Damon. "They're going to
draw fire outside. Could get hairy fast."

"Bring it on," Damon said with a grim smile.

THE FIRST VOLLEY OF gunfire near the front of the cabin
sent fear jangling through Abby. Around her, five of the six
remaining captors raced to the windows. Only Tanto, the
boyish young colt Ramon had assigned to guard her, stayed
put, though Abby could tell from the excited light in his eyes
that he'd rather be outside in the firefight.

"Take her upstairs!" Ramon barked in urgent Spanish from
his position at the front window. "Inner room."

More shots fired, to the east. A couple of Cordero's men
shifted positions. Tanto grabbed her arm and tugged her
toward the stairs. *"Ven conmigo."*

She dragged her heels, not wanting to be hidden away. Luke was out there somewhere, and there was gunfire. She needed to know he was okay.

Tanto tightened his grip on her arm at the second floor landing, making her gasp aloud. "You're hurting me!"

He jerked her with him into the hallway. Abby hadn't seen the second floor yet, though she knew there was a bathroom up here where Luke had taken a shower. She could still smell the woodsy fragrance of the soap he'd used—

Suddenly, she was jerked sideways, and two things happened in quick succession. A large hand clapped over her mouth, and a tall, muscular African-American man jerked Tanto off his feet and out of sight down the hall.

"Don't scream," Luke's voice whispered in her ear. She whirled to face him, eyes wide. He stroked her face. "Stevie's upstairs, locked in the attic. He's okay."

More gunshots sounded outside. Ramon shouted orders below, sending more men out of the cabin.

The African-American man came back alone. Abby recognized his eyes. This was Damon.

He gave her a quick look and moved toward the window looking out over the woods. "They've sent three more out there. I just took out one. That leaves two."

Abby could see Luke calculating the odds. Both he and Damon had rifles strapped over their shoulders. Luke had his own pistol, and she was sure Damon was similarly armed. She was armed, as well—Cordero's men hadn't frisked her. She hadn't had an opportunity to make her move, so the pistol had remained tucked in the holster hidden by the hem of her jacket. She pulled it out and double-checked the clip.

Luke stared at the pistol in disbelief. "They didn't search you?"

"Guess they didn't think I'd be packing."

"You're not going downstairs with us."

She touched his stubbly jaw. "I know. I'm going upstairs to protect my son."

Luke closed his hand over hers. "Don't try unlocking the door—it'll take too long and make too much noise. Just guard it." He kissed her, a long, sweet caress. He pulled away with reluctance. "Abby—"

She pressed her hand to his lips. "Save it for when I see you again."

He smiled beneath her fingers. Moving to the doorway, he checked the hallway, then looked back at her. "It's clear."

She stopped beside him, catching his free hand with hers. "Stay alive," she whispered.

He kissed her forehead and nudged her toward the stairs.

The door to the attic was closed. Abby didn't try the lock, afraid the rattle would make Stevie call out to her. The Smith & Wesson felt heavy in her hands, but she firmed her grip and settled in for as long a wait as necessary.

"How do we do this?" Damon asked.

"They're looking for intruders from outside. That gives us the advantage." Luke paused at the second-floor landing, listening. He heard two men talking in low tones.

"We could disappear. Cordero wouldn't know where to find us," one of them growled in Spanish. "I won't die for the bastard."

Luke almost felt sorry for the man. Cordero wasn't much kinder to his allies than to his enemies.

"They're at the windows," Damon murmured.

Probably looking out at the firefight still going on in the woods outside. If he and Damon could make it downstairs without much noise, they might neutralize the men without any gunfire.

They made it halfway down the stairs when the gunfire

outside suddenly halted. Luke froze on the fifth step down, almost losing his balance.

Behind him, Damon missed the next step and fell heavily against the wall with a thud.

One of the men downstairs let loose a stream of Spanish oaths. Footsteps pounded against the hardwood floor below.

Luke whirled around. "Go!"

He and Damon made it to the second floor and split up, Luke going into the first room on the right, Damon the first on the left. Luke flattened himself behind the half-open door and willed his pounding pulse to quiet down before the two remaining Cordero thugs reached the second floor.

ABBY LISTENED to the silence outside, wondering which side had won the battle. Then, a thud below caught her ear, followed by a sudden flurry of footsteps. She struggled against the urge to run downstairs to make sure Luke was okay. Stevie needed her. He was in the room right behind her, and anyone who tried to get to him would have to go through every hunk of lead she had in her possession.

There was another loud thump, then two gunshots, impossibly loud, in rapid succession. Then, silence.

*Oh God oh God oh God.*

The quiet seemed to go on forever before she heard the first soft thud of footfalls on the stairs below.

She adjusted her stance and lifted the pistol, mentally racing through the steps of her training. Strong leg back and to the side. Don't lock the arm. Weak hand supporting strong. Pad of the finger on the trigger. Squeeze, not pull.

The top of a head came into view. Then a face.

Luke's face.

She didn't relax her stance. Someone could be with him.

Luke reached the top of the stairs. "I'm alone," he said.

She could tell it was the truth. But she still couldn't lower the gun. Her limbs wouldn't move.

He reached her side and gently took the pistol from her grip. Once the weapon was safely at his side, she felt her knees buckle beneath her, and only his strong arm looping around her waist kept her from falling.

"You're alive," she whispered, gazing up into his eyes.

He touched her face, his fingers cool. "So are you."

She found her legs again. "Stevie."

Luke released her. "I need a hairpin."

"Fresh out." Abby's voice wobbled.

"Will this do?" Damon appeared on the stairs. His shoulder was bleeding, but he wore a satisfied grin. He held a lock-pick gun in his good hand.

Luke took it from him and made quick work of the lock. As Abby was about to hurry inside, he stopped her, leaning close to whisper in her ear. "He thinks he's playing hide-and-seek."

She nodded, loving him more for that one simple warning than she'd thought was possible.

She entered quietly. "I'm looking for a little boy," she called out, forcing strength into her wavery voice. She heard a soft snicker behind a cardboard box near the edge of the room. Her heart swelled with love.

As she circled the box, Stevie jumped up. "Boo!" He grinned with delight.

Abby scooped him up, kissing him wildly until he wriggled in protest. She let him go and he ran to Luke, lifting his arms.

"Again!" he demanded. "Hide again!"

Luke picked him up and met Abby's eyes over the top of their son's head, his gaze a blend of love and fear.

Cordero knew about her and Stevie now. She and Luke had nothing left to lose.

Nothing but each other.

THE BULLET DAMON TOOK to his shoulder had been a through-and-through, and the emergency-room doctor assured him the bullet hadn't hit any major blood vessels. He'd given Damon a prescription for antibiotics and painkillers and told him to follow up with his own doctor.

Damon eyed the bottle of painkillers while he waited for Quinn to answer the call.

"Heard you made a mess down there," Quinn said quietly. Damon could tell from the ambient noise that his old friend was outside in a public place. He heard shouts in Spanish in the background, and bright laughter.

"I helped clean up a mess," Damon countered, trying to keep pain out of his voice, even though his bullet wound hurt like a son of a bitch. He gave Quinn a quick rundown of what had transpired—eight of Cordero's men had died in the gun battle outside, while inside, Damon had taken out the one Abby later identified as Tanto, and Cooper had killed the one who'd shot Damon. The other man inside the cabin had fled at the first sound of gunfire upstairs, only to run straight into Aaron Cooper just outside. Two more had escaped. The Chickasaw County Sheriff's Department was out hunting for them. MacLear's crew had avoided capture.

"No sign of Cordero," Damon finished.

"He never left Sanselmo, if my contacts are to be believed." Quinn's voice didn't reveal his own assessment of his contacts' veracity. "Cooper's still in danger."

Damon grimaced. So were the woman and the kid. "What should I tell him?"

"Nothing," Quinn said. "He already knows the situation.

But you need to get to a safe place. MacLear's not gone yet. You betrayed them. They'll want blood."

Damon stifled a sigh. So much for a good night's sleep.

"I've sent someone to get you. Be ready in ten minutes. You know the safe words." Quinn rang off.

Damon hung up the phone and looked around his room at the Sycamore Inn. The bed was turned down, his clothes strewed around the room. He had only ten minutes to leave the place as if he'd never been there.

*The life you chose, my man. The life you chose.*

He tucked his arm against his side and went to work.

FROM THE BEDROOM DOORWAY, Luke watched Abby settle Stevie down for the night. After their long, eventful day, Stevie was clingy and didn't want to go to bed, but Abby soothed him to sleep with admirable ease.

She rose from the bed and motioned Luke out of the room, following him to the living room. They were staying at his parents' guest cottage, at least for tonight.

"I don't think he realizes anything strange happened today. He thought it was a game," she said quietly.

"Good." They'd taken pains to shield him from the carnage as they carried him out of the cabin and straight to Hannah's car. Abby had gone with him while Luke stayed behind for the inevitable questions.

The deputies had found the missing *Tiburones,* but so far no sign of Cordero. Sam had called his friends in the FBI and tipped them off that the drug lord might be on American soil.

"More questioning tomorrow?" Abby tried to cover her yawn.

He pulled her into his arms. "No doubt."

"I was hoping they'd get Cordero this time." She laid her cheek against his chest.

"They may yet."

She looked up at him. "It doesn't matter. I mean, it does. But it doesn't change things for us. Does it?"

It didn't. Cordero already knew about Abby and Stevie. Nothing would make a difference at this point.

They were all targets now.

But even if Cordero were still in the dark, Luke was finished playing this game by Cordero's rules.

It was time to do things the Cooper way.

"I love you, Abs," he said, not because he thought she needed to hear it but because he needed to say it.

She smiled. "I know."

"And I'm not letting either of you go."

"I wouldn't let you." Her chin rose defiantly.

He chuckled. "About what I figured."

She rubbed her cheek against his chest. "We tell everyone the truth about Stevie, right?"

"Hell, yeah. He's my boy." Luke kissed her nose. "And you're marrying me, because we're not big on the whole living-in-sin thing around here."

She gave him a miffed look. "We're not big on it in Texas, either, buster."

"No expensive rings, no fancy gown or tuxedos—"

"No big crowd."

"My family's a big crowd."

"Okay, a big crowd, but only your family. And the Langstons." She looked wistful. "They missed the first one."

"My family and the Langstons," he agreed. "And soon."

"Very soon." Her hand dropped to his butt and squeezed. "Hey—can we practice the wedding night now?"

He scooped her up, his ears ringing with her delighted laughter, and carried her to the master bedroom. "I believe in lots of practice," he murmured as he laid her on the bed.

Giggling, she pulled him onto the bed and rolled on top of

him, her arms circling his neck. She gave him a quick kiss, then pulled back, her expression suddenly serious. "I love you, too, Luke. I think I always have."

He rolled her over until she was pinned beneath him, her body warm and welcoming against his. His whole body quickened in response.

"I know," he said, and kissed her again.

* * * * *

COOPER JUSTICE *continues next month.*
*Look for Aaron Cooper's story,*
*BACHELOR SHERIFF,*
*wherever Harlequin Intrigue books are sold!*

# Silhouette *Desire*

## COMING NEXT MONTH

### Available September 14, 2010

# LARGER-PRINT BOOKS!

## GET 2 FREE LARGER-PRINT NOVELS

## PLUS 2 FREE GIFTS!

HARLEQUIN®
INTRIGUE®

### Breathtaking Romantic Suspense

**YES!** Please send me 2 FREE LARGER-PRINT Harlequin Intrigue® novels and my 2 FREE gifts (gifts are worth about $10). After receiving them, if I don't wish to receive any more books, I can return the shipping statement marked "cancel." If I don't cancel, I will receive 6 brand-new novels every month and be billed just $4.99 per book in the U.S. or $5.74 per book in Canada. That's a saving of at least 13% off the cover price! It's quite a bargain! Shipping and handling is just 50¢ per book.* I understand that accepting the 2 free books and gifts places me under no obligation to buy anything. I can always return a shipment and cancel at any time. Even if I never buy another book from Harlequin, the two free books and gifts are mine to keep forever.

199/399 HDN E5MS

Name _____ (PLEASE PRINT)

Address _____ Apt. #

City _____ State/Prov. _____ Zip/Postal Code

Signature (if under 18, a parent or guardian must sign)

Mail to the **Harlequin Reader Service:**
**IN U.S.A.:** P.O. Box 1867, Buffalo, NY 14240-1867
**IN CANADA:** P.O. Box 609, Fort Erie, Ontario L2A 5X3

Not valid for current subscribers to Harlequin Intrigue Larger-Print books.

**Are you a subscriber to Harlequin Intrigue books and
want to receive the larger-print edition? Call 1-800-873-8635 today!**

* Terms and prices subject to change without notice. Prices do not include applicable taxes. N.Y. residents add applicable sales tax. Canadian residents will be charged applicable provincial taxes and GST. Offer not valid in Quebec. This offer is limited to one order per household. All orders subject to approval. Credit or debit balances in a customer's account(s) may be offset by any other outstanding balance owed by or to the customer. Please allow 4 to 6 weeks for delivery. Offer available while quantities last.

**Your Privacy:** Harlequin Books is committed to protecting your privacy. Our Privacy Policy is available online at www.eHarlequin.com or upon request from the Reader Service. From time to time we make our lists of customers available to reputable third parties who may have a product or service of interest to you. If you would prefer we not share your name and address, please check here. ☐

**Help us get it right**—We strive for accurate, respectful and relevant communications. To clarify or modify your communication preferences, visit us at www.ReaderService.com/consumerchoice.

HILP10R

# HARLEQUIN®

## A *Romance*

## FOR EVERY MOOD™

Spotlight on
## Heart & Home

Heartwarming romances
where love can happen
right when you least expect it.

See the next page to enjoy a sneak peek
from Harlequin Superromance®,
a Heart and Home series.

CATHHHSR10

*Enjoy a sneak peek at fan favorite Molly O'Keefe's
Harlequin Superromance miniseries,*
THE NOTORIOUS O'NEILLS, *with*
*TYLER O'NEILL'S REDEMPTION,*
*available September 2010
only from Harlequin Superromance.*

Police chief Juliette Tremblant recognized the shape of the man strolling down the street—in as calm and leisurely fashion as if it were the middle of the day rather than midnight. She slowed her car, convinced her eyes were playing tricks on her. It had been a long time since Tyler O'Neill had been seen in this town.

As she pulled to a stop at the curb, he turned toward her, and her heart about stopped.

"What the hell are you doing here, Tyler?"

"Well, if it isn't Juliette Tremblant." He made his way over to her, then leaned down so he could look her in the eye. He was close enough to touch.

Juliette was not, repeat, *not* going to touch Tyler O'Neill. Not with her fingers. Not with a ten-foot pole. There would be no touching. Which was too bad, since it was the only way she was ever going to convince herself the man standing in front of her—as rumpled and heart-stoppingly handsome now as he'd been at sixteen—was real.

And not a figment of all her furious revenge dreams.

"What are you doing back in Bonne Terre?" she asked.

"The manor is sitting empty," Tyler said and shrugged, as though his arriving out of the blue after ten years was casual. "Seems like someone should be watching over the family home."

"You?" She laughed at the very notion of him being here for any unselfish reason. "Please."

He stared at her for a second, then smiled. Her heart fluttered against her chest—a small mechanical bird powered by that smile.

"You're right." But that cryptic comment was all he offered.

Juliette bit her lip against the other questions.

*Why did you go?*

*Why didn't you write? Call?*

*What did I do?*

But what would be the point? Ten years of silence were all the answer she really needed.

She had sworn off feeling anything for this man long ago. Yet one look at him and all the old hurt and rage resurfaced as though they'd been waiting for the chance. That made her mad.

She put the car in gear, determined not to waste another minute thinking about Tyler O'Neill. "Have a good night, Tyler," she said, liking all the cool "go screw yourself" she managed to fit into those words.

*It seems Juliette has an old score to settle with Tyler.*
*Pick up TYLER O'NEILL'S REDEMPTION*
*to see how he makes it up to her.*
*Available September 2010,*
*only from Harlequin Superromance.*

Copyright © 2010 by Molly Fader

HSREXP0910

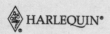

# HARLEQUIN®

# INTRIGUE®

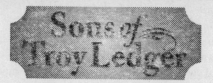

*Five brothers, one mystery*

# JOANNA WAYNE

brings an all-new suspenseful series of five
brothers searching for the truth behind their
mother's murder and their father's unknown past.

Will their journey allow them
to uncover the truth and open their hearts?

Find out in the first installment:

# COWBOY SWAGGER

*Available September 2010*

Look for more
SONS OF TROY LEDGER
stories coming soon!

www.eHarlequin.com

HI69495

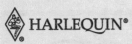

## HARLEQUIN®

### *American ★ Romance*®

# TANYA MICHAELS
## Texas Baby

Babies
&
Bachelors
USA

Instant parenthood is turning Addie Caine's life
upside down. Caring for her young nephew and
infant niece is rewarding—but exhausting! So when
a gorgeous man named Giff Baker starts a short-term
assignment at her office, Addie knows there's no time
for romance. Yet Giff seems to be in hot pursuit....
Is this part of his job, or can he really be falling
for her? And her chaotic, ready-made family!

**Available September 2010
wherever books are sold.**

## "LOVE, HOME & HAPPINESS"

**www.eHarlequin.com**

HAR75325

# HARLEQUIN
## *Ambassadors*

### *Want to share your passion for reading Harlequin® Books?*

## Become a Harlequin Ambassador!

Harlequin Ambassadors are a group of passionate and well-connected readers who are willing to share their joy of reading Harlequin® books with family and friends.

You'll be sent all the tools you need to spark great conversation, including free books!

All we ask is that you share the romance with your friends and family!

You'll also be invited to have a say in new book ideas and exchange opinions with women just like you!

### To see if you qualify* to be a Harlequin Ambassador, please visit
### www.HarlequinAmbassadors.com.

*Please note that not everyone who applies to be a Harlequin Ambassador will qualify. For more information please visit www.HarlequinAmbassadors.com.

### Thank you for your participation.

BAP09BPA